SEER TODAY, GONE TOMORROW

ADA BELL

Just when Aly finally identified her sister-in-law's killer, they got away—and they're not alone

While visiting an estate sale to pick up new items for Missing Pieces, Aly gets hit with a surprise: the elderly homeowner didn't have a heart attack--she was murdered. Aly's got the evidence in her hands, and the killer is offering to sell it to her. Time to make a deal, then call the police.

If only anyone believed her. Miriam Peabody was in her 70s and appeared to die of natural causes. Police found no evidence of foul play, but Aly knows what she saw. Worse, she's pretty sure the killer has powers of their own. As she seeks evidence to support her vision, someone is watching Aly's every move. They're always one step ahead. She needs to find concrete evidence to give the police before someone Miriam trusted gets away with murder.

ALSO BY ADA BELL

Shady Grove Psychic Mysteries

Mystic Pieces

The Scry's the Limit

Sight Seering

Mystic Treasure (Book 3.5)

Seer Today, Gone Tomorrow

The Pie in the Scry

Mystic Persons

To Cassidy

Because you'd read these books even if your mom didn't tell you to.

CHAPTER ONE

EARLY MORNINGS WERE the best part of the day at Missing Pieces. Soon I would have a steady stream of customers, but right now it was just me and the type of quiet that came rarely when living with a toddler.

Shady Grove's premiere (okay, only) antique store sat in the middle of Main Street, the perfect place to watch the town wake up. The early morning rays combined with that hush you never found later in the day gave everything a magical feel.

Of course, inside the store, I stood in the presence of actual magic. My boss, Olive, read objects to find their true owner. People who shopped here wound up uniquely satisfied with their purchases.

Olive hired me after discovering that I, too, possessed psychic powers. That came as quite a shock to both of us, believe me. After years of studying science, I wasn't exactly thrilled to embrace the idea that extrasensory powers not only existed, but I had them. Like it or not, they manifested.

When I used an object, I sometimes had a vision of a prior user. Over the past year, Olive and I had been working on exploring and controlling my powers. This morning, though, I was on my own.

The store had become a well-oiled machine over the years, so opening was a breeze. Other than pulling the cash out of the safe to put it in the register and making sure my coffee cup was full, there wasn't a ton to do until eight o'clock when the early morning bargain hunters started to arrive.

My best friend Rusty knocked on the back door. I let him in, taking in his greasy black hair and the bags under his normally bright blue eyes. "Did you get run over on the way here?"

"Very funny," he said. "I've been up all night on a stakeout."

"Sounds miserable." I gestured to the pot on the back counter. "Do you want some coffee?"

He shook his head. "Nah. Let's just do this so I can go home and get some sleep."

"Sure. What do you have for me?"

Rusty worked as a private investigator, and when he needed help with a case, he often came by to get a little boost if I could give it. His bosses didn't know, so we couldn't exactly meet at his office.

"Who's your best friend?" he asked.

"You are," I said automatically. "Why does that question scare me?"

"Because I only remind you how much you love me when I bring you something you don't want," he said. "I'm really sorry about this."

Rusty pulled a blue and purple paisley scarf from a pocket of his cargo shorts.

I stiffened. "Another affair?"

"Honestly, I'm not sure. She's young and gorgeous. He's old enough to be her father. You know how it goes—his kids are mad because she's younger than they are. They've completely shut him out. Now she's acting secretive, and he's worried that he's jeopardized his relationship with his children for nothing."

"That's so sad." Although I really enjoyed using my powers for good, this was why I didn't go into PI work myself. There was a world of difference between bringing criminals to justice and catching cheating spouses. Whatever happened to romance and happily ever after?

"What do you think?" I asked.

"To be honest, she seems to care about him," Rusty said. "The way she talks about him, the way she looks at him. I haven't caught her going anywhere other than the golf course and mundane errands."

"She married him so she'd have more time to practice her swing?"

"She's starting a charity. I've never actually seen her on the course. She mostly hangs out in the dining room. But her stepchildren think she wants their father to fund the whole thing so she can fritter away their inheritance. He's worried she's hooking up with a caddy." Rusty shrugged. "I'm just hoping you can get a reading. If she is cheating, he deserves to know. If she's not, I hope they're very happy together."

A thought occurred to me. "How did you get that scarf? Did you tell your client a psychic was going to do a reading on it?"

"Don't be ridiculous," he said. "Thaddeus thought his wife was acting weird on Wednesday. I told him that, if he could bring me something she was wearing, we could use a bloodhound to trace anyone else the scarf was in contact with."

Raising one eyebrow was a skill not granted to me, so I glared at my best friend. "I'm a bloodhound now?"

"Hmmm. Not so much. Bloodhounds are wicked fast. You're more of a... well, I want to say tortoise. But it feels like I shouldn't call you that right before asking for a favor. Tortoises are smart, right? You're a smart, beautiful tortoise."

"You're a wise man. Usually." With a wry grin, I shook my head. "It's a good thing I'd be lost without you."

He pulled a paper bag from another pocket. Cargo shorts were the best. "I brought you muffins."

"I will tell you anything you want to know," I said. "Hold on to those so I don't get crumbs on your evidence."

I held out my hands, and Rusty draped the scarf across

them. I closed my eyes and breathed deeply. My powers rarely triggered when I handled an object; I had to use it in the manner intended. Since he'd given me a scarf, I wrapped it around my neck.

Instantly, Rusty and my bag of muffins vanished.

I was in someone's kitchen, a sleek marble-topped island in front of me, a stool beneath me. My hands gripped a coffee mug emblazoned with "Everything Tastes Better with Dog Hair in It." As I lifted it to my lips, I realized someone was speaking.

"I promise, this is the last time."

"Yes, it is," I said, "because the answer is no. Not happening."

"Why not?" A whine entered the tone, and I turned my head to catch the speaker. A-ha! A man of about medium height with dark hair tumbling around his chin, oval brown eyes, and an air of desperation. The feelings inside me ranged from disappointment to frustration.

With zero clues as to this man's identity, I felt pretty sure the woman in my vision was not sleeping with him. Not given the jumble of emotions.

I rubbed my temples before meeting his gaze. "We've gone over this. It's not my money."

"Thaddeus adores you. He won't care."

"I care."

"And that's why I'll pay you back," he insisted. "Listen, Tory, I've changed. My business loans are coming in soon, and I'll repay every penny. Scout's Honor."

A sardonic smile crossed my lips. "You were never a Boy Scout."

"But not because I didn't have honor."

I'd had enough. Draining my mug, I placed it on the island with a resolute thud and pulled myself to my feet. "The answer is no. No more money. We're done. I'm not coming here again."

"What if I tell Thaddeus?"

"Tell him what? He knows I've got a deadbeat brother."

"I'll tell him that you only married him for his money."

I fixed my brother with a steely glare, strong enough to make him take a step backward. "You wouldn't dare."

Reaching up, I removed the scarf from around my neck. Over the past few months, I'd gotten a better grip on how to end my visions once they started. As soon as the fabric slid away, my world returned to normal.

"Tory isn't having an affair," I said. "She's been meeting her brother. He wants money for some reason. She doesn't want to give it to him. She's trying to keep him from hounding her husband. Sounds like there's a history."

Rusty kissed my forehead. "You're amazing. That's exactly what I needed to hear. I'll think of something to tell Thaddeus. Maybe I can question the brother, get him to give a statement."

"Speaking of needing to hear, any news on Mary Towne?"

My brother initially moved here to be near his sister-in-law after his wife died. He thought my nephew should have a stronger connection to his mother's family. Unfortunately, a few weeks ago I'd learned that either Mary or her cousin might have been the ones who caused Katrina's death, and they'd both fled town. Kevin and I had been looking everywhere for them. Rusty helped in his spare time.

He shook his head. "Sorry, Aly. I've got an ear on the ground, and I'm tracking both of their credit card statements."

"I don't understand how they've avoided spending any money since July."

"They probably haven't. They might be using cash, or they could have accounts we don't know about yet. I'll figure it out. Eventually."

"Before they come back?" We believed Mary and her cousin Priscilla were involved in a plot to kidnap my three-year-old nephew that resulted in the death of my sister-in-law. I'd do everything in my power to protect Kyle from another attempt, but having some advance notice would be nice. Although like

Tory's brother, I'd never been a Boy Scout, I also believed in being prepared.

"I'm working on it. If there is anything else I can possibly do, I'll try it. Promise."

His words made me feel bad. Rusty was clearly exhausted, burning the candle at both ends. He worked long hours studying to be a private investigator, then spent his off-hours trying to help Kevin and me. I pulled him into a hug. "Sorry. I know you're doing your best."

An alarm chimed on my phone, reminding me that I had a job to do. As I shut it off, I checked the time out of reflex. Seven-fifty-nine a.m. One minute to opening.

"Sorry, I have to go," I said. "I'll text you later. Get some rest."

"No need to apologize. Thanks again for your help," he said on his way out.

"No problem," I said.

And it really wasn't. Having visions? Saving marriages? Easy-peasy. Just another day in the life of a psychic.

Rusty headed out the back while I went to the front of the store to finish getting ready for the day. Hopefully he'd manage to get a few hours sleep before he needed to be back at work.

As I turned the sign on the door to "Open" and flipped on the overhead lights in the front room, I stopped to revel in all the amazing treasures in this room. They might be just antiques to most people, but to me, they held stories. These items breathed and lived memories. They held hope and dreams and love and more. In time, I wanted to unlock all of those treasures.

Most of our early morning antiquers preferred to poke around on their own, without my interference. (Patti from the diner even said that once. I wasn't helping, she'd rudely informed me.) While they browsed, I sat on the stool behind the register, sipping my coffee and people watching.

Today's first guest was a woman with gray-streaked hair cut into a sharp bob around her face. I'd seen her around town before but didn't know her name. Usually I ran into her at the bakery. She carried herself regally. Something about her impeccable clothes and pearl necklace made me wonder if she was looking for antique furniture, and I mentally patted myself on the back when she headed off that way.

After a while the crowd thinned out, and I found myself mostly alone in the store. Other than a middle-aged woman with long, rainbow-colored hair wearing a matching poncho and perusing our antique books, no one was here.

My phone dinged with a text from my boyfriend Sam.

Good morning! I know you're at work, just wanted to say I'm thinking about you.

As always, his thoughtful messages made me smile. Dating someone in New York City wasn't easy when the train took three hours and I couldn't afford parking within about fifty miles of the city. We didn't see each other nearly as often as either of us would like.

Me: *Morning. :-) Only fifty-six hours until you're free from summer school, right?*

Sam would be graduating with his master's degree in accounting at the end of the year. Then he'd be back in Shady Grove. Home to take me on dates and play with Kyle with me and resume the odious task of keeping the books for this store, which belonged to his mother. Helping with the money stuff was my least favorite part of the job, but after seeing the way Olive had destroyed Sam's record-keeping system after he left, I'd banned her from touching it again. But it was only September, so we'd be texting a lot and seeing each other on long weekends for a bit longer.

The bells over the door chimed, jolting me out of my bliss. A medium-sized man with fawn-colored skin, longish dark hair, and an air of authority entered. Although he wasn't tall, he carried himself with a presence, taking in the room with determination. From the few lines around his eyes, I guessed he was about thirty-five.

And he was the man from my vision.

CHAPTER TWO

FOR A LONG MOMENT, I couldn't speak. As the man approached the counter, I forced my facial muscles to curve into a smile. Scaring a potential customer away wouldn't help anyone.

"Hello," he said. "Is something wrong?"

"Good morning!" I greeted the stranger with feigned enthusiasm, sternly reminding myself that he didn't intend to star in my vision. But what was Tory's brother doing here? "Can I help you?"

"Good morning," he said. "Do you have an electronics section?"

I pointed toward the near wall. "All sales are final, so if you find something you like, there's a testing station. Make sure it works before you leave the store."

"Thanks," he said.

"Can I help you find something specific?" Knowing that this man needed money made me want to follow him, but Olive told me once she had quite the security system in place. I hadn't asked for details. Sometimes, it's better not to know.

"No, I should be okay."

I eyed him until he moved out of sight.

Another woman came in looking for a vintage bridesmaid dress, which I happily helped her find. By the time she checked out, the man from my vision had returned to the front counter, holding a bunch of black plastic devices that were probably older than me.

"Did you test those?" I asked uncertainly when he placed them on the counter. A plume of dust puffed out from under the one on the far right.

He leaned closer and lowered his voice. "I actually don't need them to work."

"Okay." Picking up the first item, I rang it up, then examined it. A small, old-school video camera. Several of them. "Are you putting on a play or something?"

"No." He glanced around the room before speaking again. "I want it to look like I have a security system in place. The company coming to set me up can't get out here until after Labor Day."

Ahhhh. Interesting. Was he really waiting for the security company, or did he realize he couldn't afford to pay them after Tory rejected his request for money?

None of my business, I reminded myself sternly. I was here to sell antiques. And these were certainly antique.

As fake security systems went, I wasn't sure how effective one from the nineties would be, but if this guy wanted to give me money for something Olive probably stocked before I was born, it wasn't my job to argue. I just smiled and tapped my temple before giving him his total. "Smart thinking."

He handed over his card, then stopped and pulled some flyers from his back pocket while I rang him up. "By the way, I'm Jeff Ahn. I just opened up a pet store down the street."

"You own Paws and Effect?" One of my favorite things about Shady Grove was the pun-filled names all business owners on Main Street were required to use. A lot of businesses on the adjacent streets followed the trend. To me, it felt like the whole town shared an inside joke.

If Jeff was opening a new business, that explained why he needed money from his sister. Rents on Main Street weren't cheap. I started to suspect that my feelings toward him had been colored by Tory's frustrations in my vision. He seemed nice enough.

Then I spotted the address. "You're moving into number fifteen? I thought that was going to be a nail salon."

Rusty and I had been excited about being able to get his and hers pedicures without going all the way to Willow Falls. The next town over had more than double the population of Shady Grove and significantly more businesses for us to frequent. It was only about a twenty-minute drive, but I'd grown to like being able to walk around town instead of hopping in the car for everything. My hometown of Sacramento sprawled over such a large area, it wasn't terribly walkable. One of many reasons I preferred Shady Grove.

Jeff shook his head. "I've been in negotiations with the owners for a while. I know they were talking to someone else, but I think there was an issue with the permits."

"You mean, you sabotaged me!" The woman who had been perusing our book section came to the front, shaking her fist. Her multi-colored hair streamed out behind her. "You told them not to rent to me!"

Jeff took a step backward, holding his hands up in a gesture of peace. "I'm sorry, I don't know what you're talking about."

"Oh no? Weren't you colluding with the mayor?" Her voice rose with every word.

Stepping around the counter to put myself between them, I plastered a smile on my face. "Hi, I'm Aly. I work here. Is there a problem?"

"That man!" She pointed over my shoulder as if there might be a chorus line standing behind me. "He got my business shut down! Now I'm stuck giving manicures out of the back of my van like some common criminal."

Was that legal? It seemed like a nail salon should have access to running water. Not the point.

"Clearly, you two have some issues to work out, but this isn't the place. I'm sorry you didn't get your store. My friend and I wanted to come see you."

That mollified her somewhat. "I could give you a business card."

"Sure." We absolutely would not be getting pedicures in a van. Well, unless it was really cheap.

The woman handed me a pink business card. For the first time, I noticed her perfect nails. Long, square-cut, with not a single chip in the thick red shellac. On each finger, she'd painted a tiny rainbow, with all six stripes in perfect lines. Very impressive. Another point in favor of the van.

"Excuse me," Jeff said. "Do you have a bag for this stuff?"

Oh! My cheeks flamed as returned to the register to print his receipt. "I'm so sorry. Just sign here." I turned back to the woman. "I'll be able to help you in one minute."

"I'll come back when *he* is gone." Her eyes shot thunderbolts at Jeff as she headed for the door. "I'm not done with you, Jeff Ahn! That's my space! You can't shut me out."

The bells over the door jingled. Jeff and I stood in silence for a while, as if waiting to see if she came back.

"Interesting lady," I said as I handed Jeff his credit card and the bag holding his stuff. Then I looked at the business card still in my left hand. "Rainbow, Owner of Nailed It! Beauty Salon."

"Yeah, I don't think she likes me," Jeff said.

"Whatever gave you that impression?" I grinned to let him know that, whatever she thought, I was cool with him. "Did you know she was hoping to rent at the same spot?"

He averted his gaze. "I did. But I also know the mayor's sister owns the salon in Willow Falls, so I was pretty sure the necessary permits wouldn't come through for Rainbow. Not that I did anything to interfere. Just... I know how business works sometimes."

That was how business worked, especially in small towns like Shady Grove.

I considered Jeff's words long after he left the store. Mayor Banister apparently drew inspiration from the town's name. This wasn't the first shady thing she'd pulled since taking office. Too bad we didn't live in Serenity Hills.

CHAPTER THREE

SATURDAY MORNING, my nephew bounded into my room before sunrise with the exuberance of a thousand puppies. "Aunt Aly! Aunt Aly!"

With a groan, I cracked one eyelid open. "Good morning, sweetie."

He leaped onto my bed, causing me to jump. "The new pet store opens today!"

Oh, yes. That made sense. Kyle had been angling for a pet for about a year, pretty much since I moved in with him and Kevin. Before that, he'd only been two and didn't talk much. "It does. Do you think maybe we should go?"

"Sure!"

It still boggled my mind how, whenever he ate a lot and then slept in (because while it was six-thirty, that constituted "sleeping in" around here), my nephew woke up the next day a brand-new child. Maybe I should switch my major from biology to child development.

Nah.

Still, spending time with him every day was quite the adventure, and I couldn't wait to see where that journey carried us. Today, life was taking us back to Main Street. Kyle's birthday was coming up, and I needed him to help me pick out his gift. Working in Missing Pieces gave me plenty of time to scour the various children's items that came in, but nothing seemed quite right for Kyle. If the perfect item did come in, Olive would tell me. Meanwhile, I'd decided to look elsewhere.

The local "toy" store mostly sold comic books and video games, which would be very exciting for Kyle in a few years but didn't help me yet. But a few weeks ago his preschool did a section on animals, and he'd switched from taking care of his rock collection to begging for a pet.

After a lot of talking—way too much, really—my brother finally agreed that I could take Kyle to get a goldfish. Small, easy to keep alive, and if it died, we could replace it for about three bucks. Perfect.

Especially because part-time retail work wasn't quite as lucrative as my brother's lawyer job. A goldfish should make Kyle happy and would fit within my budget, even if I sprang for a decent-sized bowl and a cool pirate ship to put in it. Sure, my brother could easily afford a massive aquarium, but I wanted this gift to be from me.

After breakfast, we walked into town. There wasn't much parking on Main Street, especially when the tourists poured in, and today was pretty mild. We'd walk over, stop at the local coffee shop, On What Grounds?, for cookies and iced coffee (for me), then head down the block to Paws and Effect.

Any day that included a walk through town *and* time with coffee shop owner Julie was pretty exciting for my nephew. He remained sitting at our table long after we finished our drinks, looking out the window and chattering away about kids in his class.

When I reminded Kyle that we were headed to the pet store to choose a fish, he squealed with delight. He skipped ten feet ahead of me all the way down Main Street, twisting his lower body with each step as if he needed to expend double the energy required for more mundane walking.

All of a sudden, the ground jolted beneath my feet.

Kyle stopped in his tracks. I would have walked into him if I hadn't been focused on keeping my balance.

"What's this?" He pointed ahead of us to Town Square, where trees waved despite the lack of wind.

The ground moved a second time.

Having left California more than a year ago, I didn't think about earthquakes much these days. I certainly never expected to experience one here. My first instinct was to freeze, but as the movements under the sidewalk started again, training from years of school earthquake drills took over.

I grabbed Kyle's hand. "Come on. We need to find a doorway."

The used bookstore to my left would have to do. The store wasn't open because of a firecracker incident last month, but it was either take cover here or stand in the middle of the street. The two of us huddled in the doorway, close to the ground. I pulled Kyle close against me, putting my arm around his head and neck. The benches clattered against the wooden sidewalks.

Everything would be okay.

Element one was hydrogen. Element two was helium. Element three was lithium.

When things got stressful or scary, reciting the elements of the periodic table helped me calm down. As coping mechanisms went, it might be nerdy, but it did the job.

As suddenly as the movement in the ground started, it stopped. The trees remained in place, and the nausea left the pit of my stomach. I waited in case an aftershock came, but finally realized how silly we would look cowering in a doorway all day.

Slowly I stood, brushing off my pants. "Are you okay?"

Kyle nodded. "I'm okay. What was that?"

"That was an earthquake."

"What's an ear take?"

His pronunciation brought a smile to my face. "It's when

tectonic plates in the earth shift, rubbing against each other. The movement creates irritation, which builds up pressure. That pressure has to be released, so it rises to the surface, making the ground move beneath our feet."

"Oh. Okay." Kyle's expression reminded me that three-year-olds aren't always looking for the scientific explanation. "I don't think I like ear takes."

"Me neither, buddy." Now that I'd finished checking Kyle for bumps and bruises, I felt okay continuing our journey. "Do you want to go get your goldfish?"

"Yesssss!" He punched one fist over his head and punched the air before taking off ahead of me again.

Paws and Effect sat on the corner of Main Street and Second Street, under a massive "GRAND OPENING" banner.

We were almost at the door when someone called my name.

Turning, I saw Amira Patel, daughter of our next-door neighbor. Mrs. Patel babysat for Kyle sometimes, and she'd become a member of our family. She also made killer chicken tikka masala, which was no surprise since she and her husband ran a popular Indian restaurant in Willow Falls.

Like her parents, Amira specialized in concoctions, but not the same type: she ran I'll Put a Spell on You, the local magic shop. I didn't know her well, but she'd been a huge help when I'd needed to learn to scry the past earlier this year.

I greeted her with a smile. "You getting a shop cat?"

"If only. No, I'm here because my dog ran away." Amira's eyes filled with tears, and she glanced away, sniffling. "She was almost ten years old, and she never left the yard. But the batteries must've died in her electric fence because I let her out yesterday morning, and she never came back."

"I'm so sorry."

"It's okay. I thought snuggling the other puppies would help make me feel better." She shrugged. "It sounds silly, but something told me I needed to come here today. Maybe the owner found her? I've learned not to question my instincts, so here I am."

My heart went out to my friend. I wanted to comfort her, but Kyle beat me to it. He took her hand and squeezed. "It's okay. Lola didn't run away. She's stuck. In a garage."

Amira's eyes widened. Her eyes darted to me before she looked back at my nephew. "That's sweet, Kyle, but it's not nice to make up tall tales."

It wasn't a tall tale, but she couldn't know that. My mind raced, seeking a reasonable explanation. Kyle had the magical power to find lost objects, but Kevin and I tried to keep it a secret. Amira knew about my powers, but not the rest of my family. Not that we didn't trust her; just that the fewer people who had that information, the better.

"What's a tall tale?" Kyle asked me.

"It's when someone makes up a story that isn't true."

"Like when you told Daddy you didn't eat all the cookies?"

My cheeks grew warm. Behind my nephew, Amira struggled to keep a straight face. "Yes, exactly like that."

"I told a short tale," Kyle said. Three-year-olds were not the best secret keepers. He turned to Amira before I could interrupt him. "I saw Lola."

"Aly?" She looked at me. "What's going on? Did you have a vision?"

I laughed loudly to cover my discomfort. "Just kidding! Yeah, I had a vision this morning. I can tell that she's stuck, but I don't know whose garage it is. Kyle, what else did I tell you about where Amira's dog is?"

Kyle frowned. "I see the doggie. She's black and white."

Amira was a pretty intelligent woman, so it didn't take her long to figure out what was really happening. She crouched down, meeting Kyle at eye level. "Where is she, sweetie?"

He met her gaze squarely. "Inside. There's a car. Shiny, red."

Amira thought for a minute. "Mr. Chang bought a new sports car after the divorce. Red, of course."

"Does he live near you?"

She nodded. "About three houses down. I'd love to ask him to let me in, but he's out of town this week. I gave him a ride to the airport so he wouldn't have to pay for parking."

"Meaning the red car is parked in the garage?" I asked.

Amira's eyes lit up. "With Lola? Oh, I hope you're right."

"Me, too," I said. Kyle had never been wrong to my knowledge, but as badly as I wanted to reassure her, I couldn't reveal his secret.

"Thank you, thank you, thank you!" Amira beamed at us while pulling out her phone. "I'll call him right now."

She tapped on the screen a few times before lifting the phone to her ear. When someone answered, she spun around. As she rushed away, the words "code for the garage" drifted back to me.

"That was nice of you," I said to Kyle. "But remember, we don't want a lot of people to know what you can do."

"Lola was sad," Kyle said. "She needed her mommy."

Since he'd done a good deed, I didn't push the issue. Kevin and I could talk later about the best way to allow Kyle to help people without making his secret common knowledge. Maybe it shouldn't be a huge deal in a town like Shady Grove, where so many magical people hung out. But as long as Kevin's sister-in-law was at large, Kyle needed to keep a low profile. She didn't know what he could do, and we never wanted her to find out.

Before Katrina died, Mary—or her cousin Priscilla, I actually wasn't clear on that point—went to Kevin's house looking for some great source of power. When Katrina realized that the power source was her infant son, she'd taken a stand to defend him. That choice got her killed. Mary/Priscilla fled without Kyle, which was a small blessing. But the two of them had popped up in Shady Grove a few months ago, pretending to befriend me before disappearing together.

I didn't know what they were planning, but until I found a way to stop them, we didn't want them within ten miles of us.

Thinking about the whole thing made my heart wrench. If life had worked out differently, Kyle's mother would be taking him to get his first pet instead of Aunt Aly. With every fiber of my being, I wished she'd gotten this day with him. Not to mention a thousand others.

My nephew tugged on my arm, drawing me away from those memories. "Aunt Aly! I want to go in now. Please."

I blinked back tears, forcing myself to focus on the moment.

"Sorry, buddy." It didn't occur to me that I'd stopped three feet from the pet store until he started dragging me toward the entrance. "Let's go."

Since we were supposed to be finding him a gift, I plastered a smile on my face and put a spring in my step. This was a happy day. It wasn't Kyle's fault his mother had died. Kevin and I were determined not to let her death overshadow our everyday lives.

The blinds across the entrance to Paws and Effect were drawn, but the outside looked homey and serene. You'd never guess an earthquake just hit. Hopefully, the animals were okay.

I pushed the handle and walked across the threshold with Kyle.

As soon as the door opened, the calm from the storefront evaporated. A cacophony of animal cries greeted us. Chaos reigned. Glass crunched under my feet. Birds squawked in their cages. Dogs barked. Somewhere, a kitten mewled.

Poor things. The earthquake must have terrified them.

The lights were on, but no one stood at the front counter. I didn't see any shoppers or workers anywhere.

"Hello?" I called hesitantly, unsure whether we should move any further. "Is anyone here?"

My nephew looked around the store and said, "This is messier than my playroom."

I had to bite my tongue to keep from laughing. "Yes, yes, it is. You know what? Wait here. There's glass everywhere. I don't want you to get hurt."

Kyle remained near the doorway while I ventured deeper into the store, still calling out for anyone who might have been injured during the earthquake. I hoped Jeff wasn't trapped, unable to cry for help. But not seeing him worried me. The store was open for business; the door was unlocked. He should have been here, or at least an employee.

Although based on what I'd seen in my vision, it seemed unlikely that he'd been able to afford help so soon.

No one stood behind the register, which was open. I glanced at the tray inside, but there was no way to tell if anything was missing. The store had just opened for business today, and who would pay cash for a pet? I saw a few bits of green, but nothing that looked unusual.

A mechanical sound drew my attention to the cell phone on the counter, half-covered by papers. That didn't make sense. Why would Jeff leave his phone here? Was he in that much of a hurry, or was he somewhere in this building?

A smear of blood on the counter made my breath catch. That shouldn't be there. Another spot was on the floor a few feet away. Following the trail, I held one hand over my mouth. There was a reason I'd decided not to become a doctor. The sight of blood made me dizzy.

With each step, I hoped whoever had been in the store prior to the earthquake was okay. Maybe there was a First Aid kit in the back room.

At the ajar back door, the splashes of blood ended. No Jeff, no pet store employee, no petty mischief-maker. No sign of anyone.

Whoever was in the store during the earthquake could be in trouble.

CHAPTER FOUR

MY EARS ROARED. Before I moved to Shady Grove, no one ever seemed to get hurt or killed, but somehow stumbling into bad situations had become a regular occurrence.

Element four was beryllium. Element five was boron. Element six was carbon.

Reciting the elements calmed me enough to take a deep breath and look around. Jeff had to be here somewhere. He wouldn't have left without his phone. He might be hurt or knocked out. I needed to find him.

My calm lasted until I realized that this didn't all look like earthquake damage. The store was far more wrecked than what I'd expect from the tremors we'd experienced, especially when all of the shelves remained upright. The animals' distress made sense, but not the extent of the mess.

Especially not the lack of other humans.

A shiver went down my spine when I realized that foul play might have happened, and I'd left my three-year-old nephew at the front door alone.

As if the universe heard my thoughts, a shriek reached my ears.

"Kyle!" The scream ripped through my throat as I bolted

back toward the front door, not caring if I ground more glass into the soles of my sandals. "It's okay. I'm coming!"

Another shriek.

I tore around an end cap full of aquariums, nearly knocking one to the ground in my haste. On the other side, I skidded to a halt.

Kyle's screams were not of fear or pain, but delight. Somehow, a small white and gray bunny had escaped its cage and found my nephew. He crouched on the floor, letting the rabbit sniff his hand. As I watched, the creature rose up on its hind legs and sniffed Kyle's face. The whiskers tickled his cheeks, and he giggled.

"Aunt Aly, I found a bunny!"

"Yes, yes you did. Where did it come from? Did his cage break?" Putting my hands on my hips, I gazed around the room. There, near the front windows, a wooden rabbit hutch lay on its side. It hadn't fared well this morning, though: The front door hung twisted on its hinges and at least one leg was broken. "There. Looks like he needs a new home."

"He can live with us," Kyle said. Before I could explain why that wasn't a great idea, he added, "His heart is beating fast."

"He's probably scared. It's nice of you to calm him down."

"I think he likes me."

Absently, I said, "He probably does. Stay here while I find out where he goes. We can't leave him roaming around this mess. He might get hurt."

The caged animals lived on shelves near the front of the store, separated by type. While Kyle held the rabbit and calmed him, I moved up and down the rows. Every time I turned a corner, I hoped Jeff would appear unharmed.

If he wasn't here when the earthquake hit, someone should notify him. Unfortunately, I didn't have his number. Rusty could probably get it, since Jeff was his client's brother-in-law, but if I was right, any number I got would only ring the device on the counter.

Picking it up, I pushed a button to bring up the screen saver. In a perfect world, the phone wouldn't have been locked and it would have told me everything I wanted to know, including exact GPS coordinates to Jeff.

Alas, this was not a perfect world. But the front did say "Jeff's phone," which at least told me to stop looking for his number. It didn't explain where he'd disappeared to, though.

"Come on," I said. "We need to make sure no one got hurt."

"I can find the bunny?"

The question gave me pause because he'd been holding the rabbit a second ago. "Where did he go?"

Kyle pointed toward the back of the store. "He ran away."

Somehow I doubted the scared animal would make another appearance before we left, but there was no reason to tell my nephew that. "Sure. Let's find him."

We made another sweep of the store together. In the back, we found a closed wooden door about three feet from the open one leading outside. When looking for drops of blood, I'd missed it, but now the shiny metal doorknob jumped out at me. It could be a bathroom or a closet or even a basement.

Hopefully, I knocked. "Hello? Jeff? Are you in there?"

No answer.

"Aunt Aly, I have to go potty," Kyle said.

This was why most detectives didn't have three-year-old sidekicks.

Since Missing Pieces had a bathroom in the back for employees, it made sense this place would, too. Reaching forward, I turned the knob. We were in luck!

While Kyle was doing his thing, I scoured the rest of the back. Not only did Missing Pieces have a bathroom in the back, we had a storage room. This place wasn't exactly the same but it was close enough. To my left, a stack of empty cardboard boxes had been folded neatly and set against the wall beside another closed door. That had to be it.

After I helped Kyle wash his hands, we went to the door together. No way was I leaving him alone again.

The unlocked door opened to reveal a small, square room full of stuff. A storage area, as expected.

"Jeff?" I called.

No answer.

"Bunny?" Kyle said. "Here, bunny."

Also no answer.

We ventured inside, walking around enormous bags of cat and dog food. Birdseed. Kitty litter. There were also some stacked cardboard boxes, mostly unopened. The one I peeked in contained a pile of leashes. One stack of papers lay on top of another, and I picked it up. An invoice. Not paid. Ah, well.

Since Jeff clearly wasn't in this room, I herded Kyle back to the front of the store. We needed to lock up and get out of here. If Jeff was in trouble, I should alert the police. It wasn't until we neared the door that the missing rabbit reappeared. It sat on the floor, ear cocked as if listening to the other animals. When we approached, he sat back on his haunches and looked at us.

"Can I have the bunny, please?" Kyle asked.

"While I appreciate the use of your manners, sorry, no," I said. "We'll come back for your goldfish, but let's put the bunny somewhere safe first."

Plenty of broken glass and wood chips littered the floor among the other debris, but I didn't have the first clue where to stash this rogue rabbit. Maybe it had been in an aquarium? Admittedly, while I liked animals, I'd never given a ton of thought to rabbit housing.

"Where does he go?"

That was the question. I didn't see an empty hutch anywhere. My nephew's power lay in finding lost objects, not in touching a lost object and seeing where it should go. That was Olive's wheelhouse. Holding the rabbit, to my knowledge, wouldn't tell him anything unless the little guy had misplaced his favorite carrot.

"I'm not sure, buddy. We can't let him roam loose, though. He could get hurt. Let's get him in a cage and maybe see if he wants some water? I bet he's terrified from the earthquake."

No need to let him know that I suspected something worse had happened here.

Kyle nodded. Trying to take a scared animal from him made no sense, and the rabbit seemed to like my nephew, so I ran down the rows and grabbed the first rabbit hutch I saw. Bags of wood chips lined the other side of the shelf. Water bottles and food dishes sat on the opposite side, along with food. It didn't take me long to get everything together and go back to the front.

"Here. Put him inside, and I'll fill up his water."

At the sound of my voice, the bunny startled from where it had been half sleeping. It jerked out of Kyle's arms. He yelped.

"Are you okay?"

"Bunny scratched me." Kyle's voice wavered as he held his arms out, revealing a long mark along the left one. Beads of blood already formed on the surface.

Stay calm. Stay calm. My mind raced. We needed iodine. Element number seventeen. Not nearly as good as any over-the-counter medication.

"I know. I'm sorry," I said, eyes flicking frantically around the store. Chances were that the pet store owner had medical supplies for pets or a first aid kit. But Kyle was hurt and scared and we didn't have any business poking around without Jeff.

Missing Pieces was only a block or so down Main Street. It shouldn't take more than a second to run to the section with dog beds and grab a blanket to wrap around Kyle's arm. We headed that way, temporarily leaving the rabbit's new home near the register.

Bells jingled, like the ones we had over the door at Missing Pieces. I jumped about ten feet before gathering my wits. "Jeff? Is that you?"

"Hello? Is anyone here?"

It didn't sound like Jeff's voice, but I'd only met the guy once, other than in my vision. Kyle and I inched toward the front of the store.

Out of sight, the rabbit screeched. A dog growled, and something hissed. One by one, the other animals joined in.

"Bunny!" Kyle yelled, his wound temporarily forgotten. He took off around the corner and out of sight.

Darn it, toddlers moved too fast.

"Kyle. Stop!" My voice echoed off the walls but did nothing to slow my nephew's race away from me. Heart pounding, I tore after him.

Even after a year of chasing that kid around, I was no match for him. I might be in okay shape, but he had long legs for his size, and he was powered by whatever radioactive element ran through toddler blood. By the time I skidded to a halt near the front display, Kyle stood with his hands on his hips, yelling at a guy about my age.

"Leave bunny alone!"

The guy's lips twitched. Our eyes met, and I realized that he looked vaguely familiar. Close-cropped coppery hair, a goatee with a little more blond in it than red, blue eyes. He wore jeans and a NY Yankees sweatshirt. He should have been good-looking but his fake, teeth-baring smile made him look more like an apex predator. Cold, calculating. With effort, I suppressed a shiver.

Whoever this guy was, the animals didn't like him, either. Nearby the bunny stood on his hind feet, screeching. Behind us, at least a dozen dogs barked out a chorus. Animals typically had good instincts about people. If they didn't trust this guy, neither did I.

I put my hands over Kyle's ears. To the stranger, I said, "Please move toward the front door. I think you're upsetting the animals."

He didn't move, but then he probably couldn't hear me since he'd covered his ears. Lucky. I needed four hands to get mine and Kyle's. I nodded in the direction of the exit. The stranger moved away from the animals, back toward the front door. The screeching died down, and I exhaled a grateful breath. The guy stepped back toward the main store, and the rabbit screamed again.

"STOP!" Kyle said. "You stop now!"

"The kid took the words right out of my mouth," I said calmly. "Maybe we should go outside. Also who are you, and what are you doing here?"

Keeping one eye on the row of dog cages, the guy moved in a large circle toward the rows of merchandise. When he stood on the other side of me and Kyle, he said, "I'd ask you the same question, but I already half know. You're Aluminum Reynolds."

"Aly." My eyes narrowed. "Do I know you?"

He shook his head. "I don't think so. I graduated Maloney College last spring. Brad Stephens was my lab partner. Hey, didn't you accuse him of murder?"

Fire rushed to my face. "Um, no. That's not exactly what happened. What are you doing here? And what's your name?"

"Sorry, where are my manners?" He stepped forward, hand outstretched. "TJ Crews, *Shady Grove Sentinel*."

The only newspaper in Shady Grove changed its name every few months, for reasons known only to the owner. It used to be the *Gazette*. Whatever name they went by, the paper had an office over on Second Street, not far from Kevin's law firm. Last time I checked, it was run almost entirely by an elderly woman named Ethel and this guy Hal who looked like a used car sales-man. Loud plaid jackets and everything.

Kyle squinted up at him. "You have hair in your nose."

"That's a sign of vir—"

I cleared my throat loudly.

"—being really smart," he finished.

"Are you sure you should be here?" I asked.

TJ shrugged. "I have as much right as you."

That wasn't disputed, since Kyle and I had no business

being here alone, either. But this guy gave me a bad vibe. Time to head out. As much as I wanted to find Jeff and make sure he was okay, my nephew came first.

"We were shopping," I said. "Then we found this mess, and the owner isn't here. I was just about to call the police when you came in."

"Don't worry about it," TJ said. "Take care of your nephew. I'll call them."

This guy didn't seem like the helpful sort, but it wasn't worth arguing with him when Kyle needed his arm tended to. With a smile that hopefully didn't look forced, I thanked TJ before turning back to Kyle.

"Come on, let's see if Olive has a dinosaur bandage for your arm."

"Rawr!!" With a yell, Kyle threw his arms over his head and ran for the door.

Although I hated to leave the animals with someone who clearly distressed them, we couldn't stay. As we headed out the door, I threw a glance back over my shoulder at TJ. He stood surveying the mess, hands in his pocket.

"Don't forget to call," I said. "The owner could be in trouble."

"I know. Go. I've got this."

Kyle was still on the move. Main Street didn't get a lot of traffic, but I couldn't leave him to run off on his own. I took off after my nephew, making a silent promise to come back and see what TJ was up to.

CHAPTER FIVE

BETWEEN RAISING a child to adulthood and being married to a self-defense expert, Olive was a whiz at patching up wounds. She got Kyle a dinosaur Band-Aid and promised to watch him until I got back. My nephew was so busy practicing his roars with Olive, he barely noticed me leaving.

It didn't take long to return to Paws and Effect. The sheriff's department hadn't arrived yet, so either they were unconcerned or TJ hadn't actually called them. I'd give them a little more time to show before making the call myself. I wasn't sure whether to be concerned or relieved that TJ had vanished.

Once inside, I looked for any document showing Jeff's home address. He wasn't in the store, but since his phone was, I assumed he'd been here when the earthquake hit. What if he'd gone home to tend his injuries? Or had been running late and hadn't left for work yet? I wanted to swing by his house to return his phone and assure myself everything was okay.

My mind kept going back to the drops of blood between the cash register and the door. There weren't any cars parked outside, and I hadn't seen anyone in the alley, so where had he gone? Why wasn't he back yet? I was getting more worried about Jeff by the second.

The documents I'd moved off the phone earlier turned out to be a giant stack of mail. Lots of mail, most of it unopened. On the bottom, I found a couple of letters made out not to Paws and Effect or Jeff Ahn, Owner, but just Jeff. With an address I recognized as being a couple of blocks from Rusty, in the new townhome community. All the streets there were named after trees. Shady Willow, Shady Oak, Shady Maple.

After I snapped a picture of the address with my phone, I piled the envelopes back more or less the way I'd found them. A flyer stuck out, catching my eye. Apparently we had a new local vet. Dr. M. Younger. Interesting. One of Kevin's anti-dog arguments was that the nearest canine medical provider was in Willow Falls, too far if something went wrong. What would he say if I brought home a dog and an address for a veterinarian in Shady Grove?

Before leaving again, I wanted to make sure the animals would be okay. Most of the cats had food and water in their cages. As I walked around, I patted the ones who would let me, hoping to calm the poor creatures. The earthquake terrified everyone. Using food from the back room, I also topped off all the dishes, because there was no way to know when someone would return. The dogs immediately wolfed down the food I put before them, which gave me a pang. I didn't want to make them sick, but they seemed starving. Maybe I should call someone.

Back to the register to get the vet's phone number. After I explained the situation, Dr. Younger assured me that a lot of dogs ate like they hadn't seen food in months, even when regularly fed, and that they didn't free-feed the way cats did. She also said they'd probably be fine until morning, even if there would be quite a mess for Jeff to clean up once he returned.

With her guidance, feeding the rest of the animals didn't take long. She even promised to stop by the next day to check on them.

"Anything else I can help you with?" Dr. Younger asked when the last animal was eating.

"Actually, yeah," I said. "We found a rabbit running loose around here. The back door was open, so I don't know if he came in from outside. What do I do with him?"

"Where is he now?"

"I got a hutch, but I'm not sure where he went."

She gave me a few tips for encouraging the animal to come to me. By the time we got off the phone, I felt much better. I could manage this. I just needed to be very patient and non-threatening.

As my gaze swept the area looking for the rabbit, a flashing light caught my eye. The store telephone, still hanging on the wall, had a voice mail. I didn't remember seeing the red dot when Kyle and I were here earlier, but we could have missed it.

Taking a deep breath, I picked up the receiver and pushed the button to retrieve the message. An electronic voice asked me to enter my password. Darn it. There wasn't any chance I could guess Jeff's password. I'd known the guy for less than a day, and we'd interacted for roughly ten minutes.

But maybe, just maybe…

In the past, I had successfully used my powers to "see" someone input her password onto an electronic keypad. Granted, I'd known who she was and the ghost of her aunt was secretly helping me, but it couldn't hurt to try.

I closed my eyes and summoned a mental image of Jeff. I pictured him setting up the store, feeding the animals, and walking the dogs. Holding the concept firmly in my mind, I mimed typing in a code.

"Please enter your password," the voice said again.

It jolted me out of my concentration. I took a deep breath and raised my right hand a second time to touch the keypad.

"Your time is up," the electronic voice informed me. "You have been disconnected. Goodbye."

Oh, fluorine. (I was trying not to swear. Kyle repeated *everything*.)

Invoking a vision wasn't the answer. I supposed I could try typing in random words like "dogs" and "cats" and "fish", but I didn't want to be here all day. Or I could move on. It was probably just an automated message that Jeff's car warranty was about to expire.

Where could he have gone? I gazed around the store again, but no clues jumped out at me.

"Jeff?" I called hopefully.

I didn't expect an answer, and I didn't get one.

Still, something stopped me from leaving. I moved through the store again, calling his name. If he had been knocked out in the chaos following the earthquake, he might just now be coming to.

When my search found nothing, I went to the front of the store to call the Shady Grove Urgent Care Center to see if Jeff had checked in for treatment after the earthquake. We weren't big enough for a full hospital. As expected, they couldn't tell me anything about whether a man arrived with an injury because I wasn't a relative.

As I was about to hang up, the nurse said, "But I can tell you every detail of today's episode of *As the Hospital Guides Our Lives*. What a great show."

I smiled to myself as I put my phone away. If the nurse was watching TV, it must be a slow day. Assuming the Willow Falls hospital wouldn't tell me anything, either, I decided not to bother calling them. Time to get back to Kyle.

As I turned to leave, my gaze landed on the security cameras mounted in each corner. For a second I got excited, then I remembered Jeff bought a fake system to scare away burglars. Was he expecting trouble or just being cautious?

Based on what Jeff told me, the cameras weren't hooked up to anything. But maybe I didn't need recorded footage to watch what they saw. If I could get close enough to the cameras, maybe I could induce a vision of whatever happened here.

If this worked, I'd have to check every camera in the place. I wasn't sure what area of the store to focus on. But since each one was equally likely to provide useful information, it didn't matter where I started. I went for the one nearest the back door first, thinking that it might tell me if Jeff—or anyone else—had left that way. He hadn't come out the front unless he'd been gone before the earthquake hit. Kyle or I would have seen him.

That possibility hadn't occurred to me earlier, and now it made me pause. What time did Jeff arrive at work this morning? The store might have been ransacked before the earthquake hit. The idea that he might have been missing longer than I'd initially assumed made me nervous.

As badly as I wanted to believe that he'd taken an unexpected trip to the Adirondacks and would return safely, Jeff didn't seem like the type of guy to abandon his animals. Not after he went through all the trouble of putting up fake security cameras to deter thieves. Why set all this up if he planned to take off?

Were the cameras really to deter thieves? Maybe Jeff was worried about something else, like debt collectors. He definitely didn't have money. Did he owe anyone besides his sister? I went back over our conversation in my head, but couldn't come up with a single clue. Back to the cameras.

The ceiling was about eight feet high, which put it well above my head. My eyes landed on the shelves lining the far wall. They didn't go all the way up, but might get me close enough to get a hand on the camera. I went to the corner and put my foot on the second shelf.

Something slammed into the back of my knee. I narrowly avoided hitting my head on the shelves. My heart pounded. Then I caught myself and looked around. What had happened? No one was around. Nothing for anyone to have thrown at me.

The rabbit sat on the ground, gazing up at me. Had he attacked me?

That didn't make any sense. Why would he do that? I was nice to him!

I started to climb the shelves a second time. The rabbit raced forward and grabbed my shoe.

This was getting ridiculous.

Bracing myself on the shelves, I shook him loose, being careful not to hurt the poor thing. The standing unit shifted, coming away from the wall.

What the...?

Letting go, I walked around, checking the unit from bottom to top. It wasn't attached to the walls. Without heavy items on the bottom shelf to anchor it, the whole thing would have toppled over on me. I could've broken my leg.

"Uh, thanks, little bunny?" I looked around, but the creature had once again scampered away. Probably just a coincidence. Either way, he'd prevented me from making a huge mistake. This time, I went to the storeroom and found a ladder. Setting it up near the corner got me within an arm's reach.

Resting my hands on the top of the ladder, I closed my eyes and reached for the camera with my powers. Nothing happened. I leaned over and put one hand on the record button. At this distance, I could plainly see there was no cord connecting anything, so I pulled it off the wall. Holding the camera up to my eye, I took a deep breath, turning my vision inward to locate my psychic ability. Then I pointed the viewfinder at the scene below me and pushed the record button.

Nothing happened. Darn it. Play didn't work, either. Neither did fast forward or rewind, although I didn't expect those to. Power? Nope. No batteries, of course, but worse—no vision. Another bust.

This was so annoying. Here I'd thought I'd been getting pretty good control of my powers. I was really happy to use

Tory's scarf effectively to target my vision where I needed it to go. Sometimes, I got random images. If I was learning to focus my powers, why couldn't I get anything now?

I fought the urge to hang my head and leave. Things would be okay. Maybe I hadn't learned as much as I thought. That didn't mean I couldn't find something useful.

Even though my spirits were low, I repeated the same process with the other fake video cameras, replacing each one on its mount after I finished. None of them told me anything. What good were these powers if they couldn't help me figure out what was going on?

With a sigh, I put the ladder away and returned to the front of the store. Maybe it was better to leave this one to the police. They had resources and investigative abilities that didn't rely on half-formed psychic powers. I had Kyle's birthday party to finish preparing and an exam to study for and no business investigating someone who may or may not have been kidnapped by loan sharks. Or injured in an earthquake. Time to go.

Near the exit, the rabbit reappeared, sitting on the counter near the cash register. I jumped about fifteen feet. "How did you get up there?"

He blinked at me, and I paused to gaze into his gorgeous brown eyes. They seemed so wise. Maybe the rabbit was trying to send me a message.

Yeah, right. He was probably either saying "feed me" or "find my owner" or perhaps "I'm not a he." But since I wasn't about to go looking for a rabbit's reproductive organs, "he" worked at the moment.

Thoughtfully, I scratched the bunny's head. "Are you hungry? I made a hutch for you earlier, but you didn't seem to want to go in. There's food. Look."

When I pointed, the bunny jumped off the counter. He looked around for a minute, sniffing the air, before heading toward the hutch I'd prepared. When I followed, the rabbit took a step into the cage, then backed out as if dancing. He let out a high-pitched wail, the most horrible noise I'd ever heard in my life.

"Are you okay?" I asked as if he could answer me.

The bunny took another step into the cage, then left, then squealed again.

"I don't know what to tell you. Your food is in there. I have to go home."

He ran to me, touched my shoe with his nose, then back to the cage.

Finally, I had an idea what this creature was trying to tell me. "You want to come with me?"

The bunny stood up on his hind feet, lifted his nose into the air, and squealed. Poor thing. I couldn't leave him all alone.

Since I was headed to Jeff's house anyway to return his phone, it probably wouldn't hurt to bring the rabbit along. It seemed weird to show up on a virtual stranger's doorstep holding his phone and a bunny, but at least I'd know the animal was safe.

"Hold on," I said. "We've got to put out a note for Jeff in case he comes back. He'll be looking for you if he's not home."

I took the rabbit's quiet mutterings for agreement despite knowing he couldn't understand me. It only took a minute to find a pen and piece of paper to leave on the register.

At this point, I almost hoped TJ hadn't called the police. Between the note and the fingerprints I'd just left everywhere, if anyone other than Rusty's boyfriend and town deputy Doug showed up, I'd have a lot of explaining to do. Yet another thing to worry about later. First, I needed to find Jeff, and he was probably at home.

Before leaving, I whipped out my phone and sent a message to the email address on the store's website, just in case.

Satisfied that nothing else could be done at the moment without talking to Jeff, I picked up the hutch and headed for the front door.

CHAPTER SIX

ON MY WAY to Jeff's house, I swung back by Missing Pieces to talk to Olive. While I'd been checking out the pet store, Kevin had picked up Kyle and taken him home. My boss was setting up a display of antique school supplies near the front windows. Old desks, a blackboard, abaci. Cool stuff.

"Thanks for watching Kyle. How was he?" I asked.

"A little shaken up after the earthquake, but he seemed fine. When did you get a rabbit?"

While I explained what happened, I set the cage on the bistro table by the front register. Maybe I'd get lucky and his owner would drop in to buy something.

Or maybe I'd win a Nobel Prize for converting metal into gold.

Olive listened patiently to everything, including my failed attempts to induce a vision showing what happened to Jeff.

"Maybe you're worried about nothing," she said. "He could be safe at home, wishing he hadn't left his cell phone at the pet store."

"True. If you don't mind, I'm going over there, actually, to check on him. If he's safe at home, there's no reason for me to worry about any of this. I can give his phone back and move on."

"I mind."

"I meant, if you don't mind me leaving work for a bit. I know my shift starts in about an hour."

"Aly…"

"I'll be careful! I just want to make sure Jeff's okay. And help a poor scared pet find his person."

Her expression softened. "What happens when you hold the rabbit? Any visions that way?"

I blinked at her for several long moments, letting the full implication of her words sink in. "I can get visions from living things?"

Oh, the potential ramifications. Before I'd started dating Sam, I'd been terrified that I might have a vision of one of his exes from using a chair in his apartment or pulling on one of his oversized sweaters. If I'd feared kissing him might invoke images of other women, I'd have run screaming in the other direction.

My cheeks flamed as Olive gave me a curious look. Not for the first time, I was very thankful her powers didn't include telepathy. Then again, she knew me pretty well, so she could probably guess where my mind went.

"Whatever you're thinking, stop," she said. "That's my son, and I don't need the visuals."

"Me, neither," I muttered.

"To be honest, I don't know if you can get a vision from holding a living creature. With people, I would assume not. After all, you spend hours every day with Kyle, right? Bathing him, feeding him, hugging him?"

"Chasing him, mostly." I laughed. "But yeah. He likes about seventeen hugs and kisses before bed."

"Then I'm guessing you aren't likely to have visions based on contact with people," she said. "If you could, it seems like you may have already seen Katrina's death from his point of view. After all, he was in the house when it happened."

"Yes, but based on what I saw in the mirror, he was in his room. Katrina had just put him down for a nap. Even if he heard anything, it wouldn't be much more illuminating than what the mirror showed me."

"Are you sure? What if the killer went into his room before leaving the house? You've always wondered why they didn't take Kyle. Maybe they tried."

Whoa. Never had I considered that possibility. I'd originally assumed that any grown adult who would kill for access to a baby would then pick up the baby and walk away with him. The fact that they left Kyle made me think they hadn't realized he was what they were looking for.

Olive's gaze met mine, and she nodded as if she understood.

"One thing at a time, dear. If it's possible, one day you'll get there. Kyle is safe for now, so let's focus on the problem at hand. You want to know if Jeff is hurt or missing or just playing hooky."

"Playing hooky on the day his store opens?"

"I agree it's unlikely. That's why I'm helping," she said.

"Right. Then I suppose we should get this over with," I said. Crossing the room, I opened the door to the cage and spoke softly. "Hey there, do you want to come out and play with me for a bit?"

The rabbit gave me a derisive look.

"Maybe he only answers to his name," Olive suggested.

"How am I supposed to guess that? Rabbits don't wear collars." I studied the creature up and down. "What do you think of…. Steve?"

He just looked at me.

"Melvin?"

"Promise me you'll let your future spouse name any children," Olive said behind me. I resisted the urge to point out that, if things progressed the way I'd hoped, I'd be marrying her only son.

The rabbit didn't seem remotely interested in any of the names I tossed out, but he inched closer to the door of the cage until I managed to coax him into my arms. When I picked him up, his tiny heart beat furiously under my hands.

Determined not to upset the poor little guy further, I let him sniff around my neck for a long moment. His whiskers tickled.

"Do you see anything?" Olive said.

"No, but I haven't started yet. Hold on."

After shifting the rabbit to my forearm so he would be more comfortable, I closed my eyes and reached for my magic. Nothing happened. I imagined Jeff caring for the bunny, feeding him, putting him in a luxury hutch, the rabbit equivalent of a suite at the Plaza.

Still nothing.

After what felt like an hour but was probably about four minutes, I returned Steve/Melvin to the cage with a sigh. He made a sound that suggested his own frustration mirrored mine, although I didn't know what his problem was. The cage had a salt lick, water, and fresh newspaper to poop on. That bunny was living the good life.

"Nothing?" Olive asked.

"Nope. Nothing from the cage, either." I sighed.

"It's okay. Like I said, your powers are evolving. You couldn't know whether anything would happen unless you tried."

"True, but what now?" Although the pet store wasn't my responsibility by any stretch of the imagination, I still wanted to make sure Jeff was okay. If he was injured or in danger and I could use my powers to help him, I had an obligation to do it.

Last month, I had a long-overdue talk with my mother about the family abilities. Once I'd gotten past the fact that she'd kept such a huge secret for so many years, Mom had told me that my abilities were a gift from the universe. The only way to thank the powers that be for giving them to me was to use my abilities to help people. She'd made a good point. Whether a gift or a curse, I had this special power that no one else had. I couldn't give up just because helping was too difficult or time-consuming.

"I'm going to find Jeff."

CHAPTER SEVEN

THE SHADY OAKS TOWNHOME COMMUNITY sat about three blocks from the golf course. Since I didn't have the first clue where else he might have gone and the hospital couldn't tell me anything, checking his house seemed like a logical first step in looking for Jeff. Olive had finally agreed to watch the still-nameless rabbit for about an hour. Unfortunately, I realized after leaving the pet store that Kyle and I had walked to town this morning. I didn't have my car. The trip to Jeff's house would take about six minutes on Olive's bicycle and feel like three hours if I walked it while carrying a rabbit hutch. The basket on her bike wouldn't hold him unless I took him out of the hutch, which made no sense.

Following the map on my phone, I soon found myself in front of a townhouse identical to Rusty and Doug's except for the yellow front door (theirs was blue). Removing my helmet, I parked the bike on the sidewalk beside the mailbox. Although there was no helpful name on the side, the magnetic dog covering assured me I was probably in the right place.

Then I spotted the "Welcome You Are" doormat bearing a picture of Yoda. Remembering Jeff's *Star Wars* t-shirt from earlier, this had to be it.

I strode to the door and knocked loudly, firmly. One, two, three, four. Then I listened. The only sound was a distant rumble of thunder. Shivering, I wrapped my arms around myself and sent Jeff a silent message to come open his door before the skies opened.

Still nothing. I never knew how long to wait in these situations. Silently, I recited the first forty elements of the periodic table. When no one answered, I pushed the bell and knocked again. If Jeff were here, he'd soon realize that I wasn't leaving until he answered.

By the time I reached element 108, I realized Jeff wasn't coming. Either he wasn't home, he didn't want to talk to me, or he couldn't get to the door. After seeing the state his pet store had been left in, I feared it was the first or third. But what to do next?

As if moving of its own accord, my gaze went to the shiny brass doorknob.

This was Shady Grove. No one locked their doors. My lawyer brother didn't lock our doors, and he had a hundred-thousand-dollar sports car in the garage. Well, he started after his former sister-in-law and her cousin broke out of rehab, but they were witches who wanted to kidnap Kyle. Against them, locks didn't even make sense, but I didn't point that out to Kevin because it made him feel better.

If Jeff were missing, I should leave it up to police to find him. On the other hand, if he wasn't, he wouldn't appreciate me sending Sheriff Matthews knocking on his door. Besides, on TV, police didn't investigate until someone was missing for like two days. Even if I filed a report right now, by the time they started looking for Jeff, it might be too late. The blood splashes suggested he could be in trouble, and the longer we waited to find him, the worse it could get.

Scientists were really good about rationalizing things we wanted to do anyway, and I'd just finished a research techniques elective summer course. Oh, that was it! I wasn't snooping. I was gathering evidence. Testing a hypothesis. Studying, even.

With a glance around that hopefully didn't appear too suspicious, I reached for the knob. As expected, it turned easily in my grip. I paused, waiting for a security alarm to sound but if Jeff had one installed—well, that would be way more expensive than locking his doors.

I stepped inside and shut the door behind me, leaning back against the cool wood while my heart calmed a bit.

The entryway contained a short tiled hallway with a staircase leading upward and a living room ahead. It looked exactly like Rusty's house but in reverse. Before moving another inch, I called Jeff's name repeatedly. When no one answered, I finally pried myself away from the door and headed into the living space.

In stark contrast to the pet store, Jeff's townhouse was spotless. Not a dirty dish or crooked throw pillow in sight, no dust on the books lining the shelves, remotes lined up perfectly on the wooden coffee table. There were even vacuum lines on the rug. It was exactly as clean as I would leave a place if I wanted to avoid leaving any evidence after abducting its owner.

Possibly, I'd been doing too many Netflix viewing parties with Sam late at night. We liked the murder mysteries, but maybe it was time for us to try a good romcom instead.

My eyes fell on a laptop sitting at a ninety-degree angle to the remotes. A voice in my head, which sounded remarkably like Kevin, told me not to touch it. I'd invaded a man's privacy enough for one day. But Jeff was injured, possibly missing. He couldn't answer his phone. I needed to make sure he was okay. If the laptop could tell me where to find him, I had to try.

Crossing my fingers that it was unlocked, I used a tissue to lift the lid and perched on the edge of the couch. Thankfully, he'd left himself logged in, so I didn't have to try to guess a password. As much as I needed more practice in that area, I preferred to be able to access the information I wanted. Pulling up a browser window, I quickly found a link to his email, which was also logged in. Excellent.

Yes! An email!

The unread messages notification brought a smile to my face. Maybe this was it. I could barely breathe as I clicked on the inbox. Several emails popped onto the screen, and I scrolled eagerly to the end of the list. My heart pounded.

It was from me.

The message I'd sent from the pet store not thirty minutes ago sat at the end of a long line of benign inquiries. That was it. Other than mine, the most recent one asked about the store hours. It had been sent at nine-fifteen this morning. Jeff's reply told me nothing other than that he'd planned to be at the pet store during the posted business hours. I could have guessed that.

Wait! The IP address. That would at least show whether Jeff was here or at the store when he sent the response. Theoretically.

A glance at the email headers told me that nearly all of the messages sent came from one of two locations. Popping both into an online IP search engine told me they originated in Shady Grove, New York. Super helpful.

Before I could stop to think about what a bad idea this was, I sent myself an email from Jeff's account. Then I pulled it up on my phone to compare the data. The number didn't match the one on the nine-fifteen email. I suspected that meant Jeff sent it from Paws and Effect, which made it likely he was there at nine-fifteen this morning.

Feeling motivated by my small victory, I wiped my fingerprints off the laptop keyboard and moved on to the rest of the house. The kitchen looked as pristine and unhelpful as the living room. Not a single dish on the counter, everything clean, not so much as a fingerprint on the shiny stainless-steel dishwasher and fridge. Jeff clearly did not live with a three-year-old.

Also no sign of a pet. No dog or cat wandering around, no

food dishes, leash, or cat box. I'd have expected a person who ran a pet store to have some animals in his home. Ah, well.

Out of curiosity, I put my hand on the coffee pot to see if happened to still be warm, but no. Then I grabbed a mug from the cupboard and mimed pouring coffee to see if I could get a vision of Jeff getting ready for his day.

Nope, nothing. Was it possible to get a cold in my powers? I made a mental note to research whether any of the gases released by an earthquake could suppress psychic abilities when I got home.

Okay, that was pointless. He probably just hadn't had coffee this morning. Maybe he was a tea guy. The coffee maker looked as untouched as everything else.

Then I spotted a note on the counter.

Jeff—

As we've discussed, payment is due in full at the time of services. Your check was unsigned. This is not the first time we've had an issue. Please remit cash payment to me immediately.

A business card for Mellie's Maids sat at the bottom of the page. That explained the vacuum lines on the carpet. Rather than touch the card, I snapped a picture with my phone. Maybe Mellie could tell me what time she'd been here and if she'd talked to Jeff today. If they'd met so he could give her the payment, that would help me narrow down what time he disappeared.

Beneath the note, I found a stack of unopened mail. Phone bill, water bill, mortgage company, and more. Suddenly, my vision from yesterday came back. Jeff wanted to borrow money from his sister, and she refused. What had he said… Something about waiting for his loans to come in. If Jeff was having financial trouble, that gave him a reason to disappear. Or maybe someone got tired of waiting for payment. How many people did he owe?

The rest of the home told me only that Mellie provided excellent cleaning services. Maybe I should ask Kevin to hire her. The only other room downstairs was a half bath containing a stacked washer/dryer. Upstairs, a full bathroom connected two large bedrooms. No Jeff. Now that I'd found Mellie's note, I was not at all surprised to find everything spotless.

Lucky guy. Our house was desperately in need of a deep clean.

If the person doing the cleaning could give me information related to Jeff's disappearance, even better. I'd call her as soon as I left. But first, I was determined to induce a vision of virtually anything.

Beyond the kitchen was a door with a deadbolt. Must go to the attached garage. If Jeff's car was here, that would suggest he hadn't gone anywhere voluntarily. Shady Grove was small and relatively easy to walk, but once you got about half a mile outside town, there was nothing but highway in every direction.

Going to the door, I grasped the handle firmly. I closed my eyes, summoned a visual of Jeff, and disengaged the deadbolt with my other hand. Then I twisted the knob and opened the door.

Still no vision. I fought the urge to kick something. Of all the time for my powers to desert me.

Worse, the garage was empty.

To be fair, I didn't know if Jeff owned a car. No one had mentioned it yesterday, and when he came into Missing Pieces, he was on foot. But if he did, and it was gone—that supported the "Jeff ran away" theory. It was possible I was trying to locate someone who didn't want to be found. Maybe he'd staged the whole disappearance.

I walked into the garage and turned slowly in a circle, my arms spread wide. If I'd done all this only to find that Jeff went camping, I'd be so mad. But that didn't fit. The email this morning with the store hours and the fact that the store was open when I got there suggested Jeff intended to be at Paws and Effect. It was the Grand Opening. He should've been in the shop.

Something happened to him.

If I found the car, would I find Jeff? And how would I find either of them without my visions?

CHAPTER EIGHT

WHEN I PULLED out my phone, a text from Amira waited on my lock screen. She'd sent a photo of her and Lola, looking ecstatic. As happy as I was for her, I couldn't begin to answer the questions she certainly had, so I closed the message.

A quick call to the police station confirmed that TJ hadn't contacted them earlier. Definitely suspicious. The police also told me they absolutely were not going to give me any information about Jeff's vehicle. Sheriff Matthews asked if I wanted to report a missing person and then strongly suggested I keep my nose out of police business. No shocker there. As soon as we hung up, I made a video call to Rusty.

He looked much better than the last time I'd seen him, having clearly slept and showered in the intervening twenty-four hours.

"Hey, sorry to bother you, but I need your help."

"Just what everyone dreams of hearing," he replied dryly. "What's up?"

"Do you remember the brother from my vision yesterday?" When he nodded, I continued. "Turns out, he owns the new pet store in town. And a house near you. Also, he's missing."

"Whoa. Hold up. That's a lot of information at once." He

picked up a coffee cup and took a drink, savoring it for a moment before he spoke again. "I talked to my client yesterday, and yes, his brother-in-law was opening up a pet store in town. He wasn't at all surprised to hear the guy was asking his wife for money, because it's happened before. I did some digging to get a home address—it sounds like I should have just asked you."

"I got lucky," I said.

"You mean you had a vision of his home address?"

"No." I frowned at him. "I haven't had any visions since yesterday, now that you mention it. I'm starting to think something's wrong with me. I'm having to do detective work the old-fashioned way."

"You mean, talking to people?"

"Mostly, yeah. It's annoyingly slow. Listen, can you find out if Jeff Ahn owned a car?"

"You mean, can I use my super-awesome sense of sight to tell you that I see him driving around in a blue Mazda every day?" He winked at me. "Who needs visions when you have eyes?"

That was the gorgeous thing about small towns. Everyone was always in everyone else's business. I should've known anyone living in this community would recognize the other owners' cars. Especially when Rusty was working to hone his powers of perception.

"Did you see him this morning?"

"Nah, I usually pass him on my way home in the evenings. I'll let you know if I see him today."

So much for that. Although I was starting to suspect Jeff wouldn't be driving home today as usual, I thanked Rusty and let him get back to work.

Flipping to my photos, I pulled up the number for Mellie's Maids. Then I realized that the rest of my family was home. Even if Mellie were free for a last-minute cleaning, I couldn't interrogate her while Kyle and Kevin played trains three feet away. But there might be another house I could use. I switched to my texting app.

Me: *Hey. I need a favor. I'm sending a woman to clean your house.*
Rusty: *Great! What's the favor?*
Me: *Let me in?*

Three little dots told me Rusty was typing. They vanished, then reappeared. Then vanished. Nearby, a car door slammed. I jumped about three feet.

Who was coming to Jeff's house?

A male voice spoke. "Does Mr. Ahn own a bicycle?"

Uh-oh.

A second voice answered the first, one I recognized. Doug. "I'll make a note of it, but that looks like a woman's bike. Maybe a guest?"

They hadn't said they were coming here! I said I didn't want to file a missing person's report so I wouldn't get caught. Regardless, Shady Grove's entire full-time police force now stood outside. All two officers.

This was getting worse by the second. I couldn't go back through the house. There was no legitimate reason for me to be here. If Doug were alone, I'd risk the stern talking to, but as the voices drew closer, I became more certain that the first person who spoke had been Sheriff Matthews. He must have driven here as soon as we got off the phone, and he would one hundred percent arrest me for being in a missing man's house.

Okay, Aly, think.

Element 110 was darmstadtium. I still couldn't spell that. Element 111 was roentgenium.

Much better. I took a deep breath, and the room stopped spinning. The door to the house had thankfully shut behind me when I came out to the garage, so that wouldn't immediately look amiss to the officers. But where to go?

Although most people where I grew up kept their garages

crammed full of years' worth of storage, these homes only went in about four months ago. No one had time to accumulate stacks of convenient boxes for me to hide behind.

A large button beside the door would operate the overhead door and set me free. That wasn't an option, though—even if by some miracle the door was silent, I had no way to close it from the outside. The officers would see the opening when they left and put it together with the disappearing bike on the sidewalk.

Didn't most garages have a regular door leading outside in case of a fire? A-ha!

To my right, I found the exit. A windowed door opened into Jeff's side yard. I didn't have a great reason to be there, either, but it beat hanging out inside waiting to get charged with breaking and entering.

Slowly, I turned the knob. The door swung silently inward. Hardly daring to breathe, I eased it open just enough to sneak through, still not standing upright. Then I pulled it shut behind me. Freedom!

Almost.

A black iron fence circled the small, neatly kept yard. There wasn't time to search for clues, but Jeff had a well-manicured lawn, a small barbecue, and a table with chairs. While rushing toward the gate, I wondered bizarrely if he'd paid the lawn care people or if I should add them to my growing list of people to question.

Once the gate shut behind me, I breathed a little easier. I still didn't know how to get to Olive's bike with Sheriff Matthews standing on the front porch. Well, how long could they possibly be here? I could wait.

Thunder cracked overhead. A gust of wind sent a chill through me, reminding me August was a prime time for thunderstorms around here.

I could come back for the bike.

Moving away from the side of the house, I went across the small yard connecting Jeff's house to his neighbor's. While I didn't have a good reason to be there, either, at the moment, I just wanted to put distance between me and Sheriff Matthews.

After crossing to the driveway, I glanced back at Jeff's house. No sign of life. The squad car was parked by the sidewalk, but no one stood on the front porch. They must have gone inside. Not wasting any time, I broke into a jog. Rusty and Doug's place was only about two blocks away. I could wait there until it was safe to go home. And make a date with a housekeeper.

I loved efficiency, and killing two birds with one stone made me smile. But as I rounded the corner onto Rusty's street, my feet drew to a halt. Maybe I wouldn't have to call Mellie after all.

A black Ford Expedition with "MELLIE'S CLEANING SERVICE" emblazoned on one side sat in a driveway at the end of the block.

Did Mellie live in this neighborhood, too? Or was she cleaning everyone's house while she was in the area? At the moment, I didn't care.

Fueled by the adrenaline of almost getting caught, I jogged toward Rusty's neighbor's house. Then I forced myself to stop and think. I didn't know who lived there or if they'd be home. Some people might not appreciate me bursting into their home and accusing the woman from their cleaning company of kidnapping.

My mind raced as I forced myself to breathe normally. What had Rusty told me about his neighbors? They'd held a block party every time someone new moved in. He did not like ambrosia salad. Once I'd googled that, it made sense. But I wasn't sure who lived at the end of his street, and standing here sweating wasn't likely to tell me.

Trying to look nonchalant, I stretched a few times as if preparing for a jog. Then I walked down the street at a steady clip, arms swinging like I was just out for some exercise.

When I got to Mellie's van, I stood there for a minute, marching in place while I decided what to say. This was my best chance to get answers without paying a hundred bucks to get Rusty's house cleaned, and I wasn't about to let it get away.

Walking to the front door, I pushed it open and stuck my head inside. After all, fortune favors the bold. "Mellie? Are you here?"

A moment later, a tall woman with long hair pulled into a high ponytail appeared in the doorway. On her white t-shirt, large pink letters spelling "Mellie's" answered any questions I had about her identity.

"Who are you? If you're selling something, the owner isn't here," she said. "You should go."

"My name is Aly. Actually, Mellie, I'm looking for you."

Her eyes narrowed. "What do you want?"

"I'm here to talk to you about Jeff Ahn," I said. "I understand he owes you money?"

Her shoulders sagged. "I should've known someone would figure it out."

My eyes widened. She was confessing! The police were so close. I just needed her to let me go get them and wait patiently until they arrested her. But first—

"Where's Jeff?" I asked.

Mellie's face scrunched up. "Isn't he at the pet store? He better be working. That man owes a debt to everyone in town. He's going to need to sell a lot of goldfish to pay his bills."

Now I was the one who must look confused. "What are you talking about? I thought you just said you kidnapped Jeff?"

"Kidnapped!" Her eyes widened, and she shook her head vigorously. "Oh, no. No way. You're saying that mooch is missing?"

This conversation was not going the way I'd hoped. "Yes, he disappeared this morning. Either before or during the earthquake."

"What earthquake?"

"You didn't feel it? It happened around nine-fifteen."

She thought for a minute, then shook her head. "Nah, but

that's when I do Jeff's house. He's never there, so I turn up my music and dance up a storm while I vacuum."

"That's why I wanted to talk to you. Did you see Jeff when you arrived?"

"Sorry, no. Even before he got the shop going, he was always gone. You sure he's missing?"

"Pretty sure."

"Great. Now he's not going to pay me." Her shoulders sagged. "To be honest, it wouldn't surprise me if he took off."

"How much does he owe you?" Although the idea of paying for a housecleaner was way down the road for me, I couldn't imagine it cost the kind of money that might cause someone to fake an accident and skip town. "Have you been cleaning without pay for a while?"

"Oh, no," she said. "He only owes me like two hundred bucks. But there's also the house painters and the gardeners and the dealership... They towed his car, you know."

Well, that answered one question. "They did?"

"Yeah. Hooked him up right in front of the bakery. I just happened to be there. Tried so hard not to laugh."

"Weren't you worried that if he didn't have a car, he couldn't get to work?" And if Mellie didn't know Jeff was missing, what was she confessing to a minute ago? "Let's go back. You said you knew someone would figure it out."

"I meant Jeff or one of his friends." She sighed and took her hair out of its ponytail, taking a moment to reset it before continuing. Finally, she put her hands on her hips and looked me straight in the eye. "Listen. I don't want any trouble. And I certainly don't want you telling people I made that man disappear."

"I won't, as long as you tell me what happened."

She pulled a small device out of her pocket and held it out to me. "This morning, when I realized he wasn't going to pay me again, I took his Switch. You can have it back. I knew it was stupid as soon as I left."

"His Nintendo?"

"Yeah. They're expensive, but small and portable. Thought that would make him think twice about stiffing me in the future. Here, take it."

Boo. She hadn't been confessing to kidnapping at all.

I shook my head and stepped backward. The last thing I needed was for Sheriff Matthews to catch me with Jeff's expensive electronics after he saw a girl's bike outside his house. Especially when I was the one who alerted them to his disappearance. "You should return that in person. I'm just trying to find Jeff."

With a shrug, Mellie pocketed the device. "Don't know where he is, don't care. But it's getting late. I need to finish this house before my kid gets off the school bus. Morning kindergarten, you know."

With a frustrated sigh, I thanked her and turned toward the sidewalk. It was time to get Olive's bike and go back to Missing Pieces. Although I'd never met Mellie, the fact that she'd openly admitted to theft made me think she probably was telling the truth about everything else.

Unfortunately, our conversation left me with more questions than answers.

CHAPTER NINE

BY THE TIME I retraced my steps to Olive's bicycle, the police car in front of Jeff's house was gone and she'd sent me three texts about coming back to pick up the rabbit. Poor bunny had a rough day. Maybe it was time to take him home and snuggle with a good movie.

But first, there was one more person I wanted to talk to. If Jeff was missing, his sister deserved to know. Rusty had told me that Tory was using the Shady Grove Golf Club to get her charity off the ground. It seemed like a good place to find her, especially since I was already nearby.

Not for the first time, I found myself grateful Kevin had bought us a family membership after moving to town. He wanted it to schmooze clients. I'd liked hanging out by the pool with Kyle over the summer.

My vision unfortunately hadn't told me what Tory looked like. I knew she had well-sculpted fingernails and fawn-colored skin. When I got to the club, I had to ask the guy behind the front desk. Ben had been working here the entire time we'd lived in Shady Grove, but we'd never talked beyond the basic pleasantries.

"Do you know Tory Emerson?" I asked after he handed back my card.

"Yes, of course," he said. "I've worked here all four years of college. I know everyone. She's in the dining room."

Awesome. After thanking him, I stuffed my wallet back in my bag and headed toward the dining room. My stomach rumbled at the aromas coming from the kitchen. It was a little early for lunch, but maybe I could order a burger while I figured out a way to approach Tory.

I'd met my server once or twice—she was probably in her forties, her dark hair held back in dozens of tiny braids secured by a headband. She had a kind smile and sharp brown eyes. According to her tag, her name was Brenda.

As Brenda filled my water, I asked, "Do you know where I could find Tory? I heard she's starting a charity."

She looked me up and down as if assessing whether I looked capable of donating in my leggings and sweater I'd picked up on clearance. Apparently not. "Mrs. Emerson? Oh, sure. She's right over there. You planning to volunteer?"

"Yeah, something like that," I said, my eyes following Brenda's gaze. "Thanks."

No wonder her husband thought Tory was cheating. She sat in the middle of the room at a table large enough for six people. In the few moments I took to consider the best way to approach her, I watched her charm everyone who walked by.

After Brenda took my order and left, I braced myself and went over to introduce myself.

"Tory Emerson?"

She looked up at the sound of her name. "Yes. And you are?"

"Aly," I said. "I work on Main Street. I know this sounds weird, but I think something might have happened to your brother."

"To Jeff?" She snorted. "That seems unlikely. In high school, they called him Teflon Jeff. Nothing ever stuck. What's he done now?"

I swallowed and wiped my palms on my pants. I'd been prepared for a lot of reactions, but derision wasn't one of them. "He hasn't done anything, I'm sorry to tell you this, but he's missing."

"Wait a minute. Are you the one who called the police?" She rolled her eyes. "They told me they got asked to do a 'wellness check.' I couldn't believe it. Told them not to waste my tax dollars."

"But no one has seen or heard from your brother all day. Aren't you worried about him?"

She gazed at me for a long moment, unblinking. When I didn't break eye contact, she sighed and reached for her purse. "Not you, too. How much does he owe you? Normally I wouldn't do this but you seem like a nice girl and you're so young—"

"No!" The harshness in my voice made both of us flinch. Before she could respond, I said, "I'm trying to find him to make sure he's okay. No one has seen Jeff since this morning. The pet store was wrecked, his phone was left on the counter, and we can't find him."

She continued to study me. Finally, she nodded and put her purse back on the chair beside her. I felt like I'd passed an unwritten test. When she spoke, her voice was low. "Listen, Aly, I'm going to tell you something I probably shouldn't."

Eagerly, I leaned forward. "Do you know where he is?"

"No, but he's fine. My guess is, he ran away."

"But he's got a new business that just opened. He seemed in high spirits when I met him. Why would he take off?"

She sighed and shook her head. "Do you have a younger brother?"

"No, sorry. My brother is older."

"Growing up, Jeff always expected me to take care of him.

Now that we're adults, he's still constantly asking me to clean up his messes. Mark my words—you're wasting your time. He probably drove up into the Adirondacks and is staying in my husband's cabin. Without asking, of course. I told Thaddeus not to show Jeff where we kept the key. And now look what he's done."

Before she could go further down that tangent, I put one hand on her arm. "Hold on, though. I heard his car got repossessed."

She snorted. "Yeah, for like an hour. Then Soft Touch Tory got it back for him." Her tone softened. "Listen, you seem like a sweet girl. I don't know why you care so much about my brother, but listen: he's not missing. Jeff took off. He's fine."

Lovely, just lovely. I'd spent all day trekking all over Shady Grove to ensure Jeff wasn't hurt or worse, and all this time he'd been living it up in some mountain cabin.

"Does the cabin have a landline?"

She shook her head. "I can call his cell, if that would put your mind at ease."

"Thanks, but I have it. Wherever he is, he didn't take his phone with him." I hesitated, unsure how she would take my next words. "Forgive me, but you don't seem terribly concerned."

"There's no need to worry. I've been through this before, and I'm sure I'll have to deal with it again. Family, you know? But Jeff always comes out on top. Don't ruin your day worrying about him."

Part of me wondered if her utter coldness was masking something else—a sign that she'd done something to Jeff, maybe, to stop him from asking her husband for money. But she didn't seem cruel so much as resigned. If I had my powers, I'd try to get another vision off her, just to be sure.

This was so annoying. I needed my powers to fix themselves.

After thanking her, I went back to my own table just as Brenda sat down a gorgeous bacon gruyere cheeseburger on sourdough. My stomach jumped for joy. Playing detective on an empty stomach was no fun.

At least one good thing had come out of this trip. As I picked up my burger and took a bite, I realized that if Jeff simply ran away to avoid paying his debts, there was no need to keep looking. I was free to focus my attention on getting my powers back.

My clarity lasted through lunch and half the ride back to Missing Pieces to return Olive's bike and pick up the rabbit she'd now sent eleven texts about. Then, my phone rang. I couldn't talk while riding, but I recognized the vet's number, so I pulled over to answer.

"Hello? Is everything okay?"

"That's what I wanted to ask you." Dr. Younger sounded concerned. "Did Jeff ever turn up?"

I shook my head before realizing she couldn't see me. "No, but I talked to his sister. She's convinced he skipped town to avoid paying his debts."

"Really?"

"Yeah." Although the easy thing to do was write this call off as idle gossip, then hang up the phone, something stopped me. "Why do you ask?"

"It's just… How well do you know Jeff?"

"Not well at all. We met for the first time on Friday morning and spoke for all of four minutes."

"He asked me to come to the pet store on Thursday afternoon while the animals were delivered. He was very concerned for their well-being, and he wanted someone to oversee their unloading. To me, that doesn't sound like someone who would up and abandon the animals a couple of days later. I'm worried." She hesitated. "Did you get that kind of vibe off him?"

If I were being honest with myself, no, I hadn't. I'd latched onto Tory's lack of concern as an excuse for disentangling myself from all of this and focusing on whatever was happening with my powers. But my gut told me that Jeff hadn't run away.

After a long pause, I exhaled slowly. "No. I think something bad happened to him."

CHAPTER TEN

AFTER LUNCH, I went to finish my shift that should have started at ten. Olive was reasonably flexible, but a reliable employee was imperative to allowing her to have work/life balance. Shady Grove typically got a lot of tourists during the summer because of our proximity to the Saratoga race course, so we were pretty busy. Great for business, not great for learning about magical abilities.

I didn't get a chance to ask about how a person could lose their powers before it was time to go. While Olive would have approved overtime, it was my night to watch Kyle. Kevin had a date, and I had exams coming up.

It wasn't until I went to pick up the rabbit's cage that I remembered I'd walked to work that morning. It was reasonably cool when I'd left my house, but the humidity grew throughout the day. Lugging this hutch home at the end of the work day would feel like dragging a tugboat through pea soup.

"Don't even think about it," Olive said.

"What?"

"You're not leaving the bunny."

"Come on, Olive, look, he's asleep. You won't even know he's here," I argued. "It's a long walk."

"I know everything in my store. Look, you wanted to play Jane Goodall, and I support that. But my store can't smell like rabbit during one of the busiest shopping times of the year. One day was enough."

She had me there. Sensing this wasn't the best time to ask for another favor—even one that involved my powers rather than rabbit-sitting—I picked up the hutch and took it to the back. I could do some research tonight and we'd talk about my power loss in the morning.

All I wanted to do when I got home was chill out with a good movie, then go to sleep. Kyle went to bed at seven, so he wouldn't need me unless he woke up. But there were about a million questions I needed answered, and before I could even start my research, I had to get past the lion at the gate. Er... My brother.

As expected, Kevin wasn't exactly thrilled to see me arrive home with a bunny in hand. "That's an odd-looking goldfish."

"You think so? I think he's cute."

"Please tell me you didn't get a rabbit."

"I'd love to lie to you, but you can plainly see the truth." Literally. That was my brother's secret superpower, like my visions. Lies looked different to him. "I'm surprised Kyle didn't mention it."

"I'd hoped he was mistaken," he said. "Three-year-olds love to exaggerate."

"Kyle and I found him in the pet shop. He didn't have a cage or anything."

"He's got one now," Kevin pointed out. "Why didn't you leave him in it?"

Quickly I explained what happened, including the fact that the animal seemed to want to come with me. "The poor thing was so scared. Look, I know you didn't want to get Kyle a furry pet any time soon but—"

"No buts," he said. "I'm headed to Julie's. I'll take it with me. Maybe she'll watch him until Jeff shows up. I don't want Kyle to get attached."

Julie Capaldi was the owner of On What Grounds?, the local coffee shop. She and Kevin started dating after the Shady Grove Annual Treasure Hunt a few weeks ago. With their dual law degrees and love of caffeine, they made a pretty cute couple. Kyle adored Julie, and so did I. It was nice to see my brother happy again.

"You don't want to keep him? Come on, I promised the rabbit a name."

"Another word out of you, and I'll name him Aluminum." My brother knew I'd never forgiven my parents for naming me after the thirteenth element rather than, say, something a little less unique.

"Too late. His name's Kelvin," I shot back. My brother had gotten a name change when he turned eighteen. What could I say? My parents liked science.

"Don't you dare," he said.

"Too late. It's done. Come on, Kelvy," I said to the rabbit hutch as I moved toward the stairs. The animal made a muttering sound that I chose to interpret as approval.

"Aly, wait," Kevin called after me.

"Nope! The bunny has been named."

"It's about Mary."

Those words stopped me dead in my tracks. Over the past few weeks, it had looked like Kevin's sister-in-law had vanished into thin air. Not even Rusty could get any useful leads. Any news was welcome.

Setting the rabbit cage on the kitchen table, I turned to give my full attention to my brother. "Did you find her? Or them?"

"Not exactly," he said, "but there are rumblings that Mary might be back in the area."

"What happened?"

"I believe everything Priscilla told you was true: Mary had her cousin involuntarily committed, using Mary's own name.

When the two of you started talking, Mary went to the facility and signed her out. She didn't want to risk you finding out."

"Why go to all that trouble?" I asked. "Why not just have Priscilla committed as herself?"

"Good question," Kevin said. "Mary must have wanted people to think she'd been locked up."

So many questions. Mary, Katrina, and Priscilla had been besties growing up. According to one of Katrina's old friends that I'd tracked down, they were inseparable. Then Priscilla moved to Baltimore for college—Johns Hopkins, I'd later learned—and Katrina went to Columbia, where she met Kevin. When I'd scried the murder, I'd seen someone with the same tattoo they shared. Unfortunately, I didn't get a close enough look to figure out which one did it.

"Why not voluntarily commit herself?" I asked.

Kevin shook his head. "Presumably because it would limit her movements. Have you heard anything from Mallory?"

Priscilla joined the wedding party last minute after an unfortunate accident happened to another bridesmaid. It all seemed too pat, and I'd been trying to contact the missing bridesmaid to find out what really happened.

"Not yet. Do you think Priscilla caused Mallory's broken leg?"

"It's possible," he said. "She would've known all about bones."

I sighed. "I'm still trying to find her. Last night, I sent messages to a bunch of people. I was planning to check for replies when I got home."

Kevin picked up Kelvy's cage. "Then we'll leave you to it."

"Tell Julie I said hi."

The two of them disappeared in the direction of the garage. Ten seconds later, a shrieking filled the air. The loudest, most horrible noise I'd ever heard in my life, accompanied by a banging.

Make that the second most horrible: The toddler was awake.

Immediately after the ruckus started, Kyle called out for his daddy. Indecision gripped me at first, but Kyle would be fine in his room for a minute. He might even go back to sleep. On the other hand, if Kevin and the rabbit were being attacked in the kitchen, they needed me.

I dashed through the doorway.

Instantly, the shrieking stopped.

Kevin stood gaping at the cage, white-faced. He didn't appear to be bleeding.

"What happened?"

"I don't think the rabbit wants to come with me," he said. Then he gazed toward the ceiling. "I need to check on Kyle."

After he left, I eyed the rabbit carefully. "Everything okay, Kelvy?"

The bunny wrinkled his nose at me before letting out a whimper. Carefully, I took a step toward the cage. An inch at a time, I lifted my hand toward the exterior so the animal could sniff me. There was no sign of whatever set him off, but I didn't want the poor animal to freak out again. A long time ago, I'd heard of rabbits scaring themselves into a heart attack. It seemed impossible, but what did I know? Now that we'd taken responsibility for this creature, I needed to protect him.

He sniffed my hand, then rubbed his cheek against my fingers through the cage. "Everything's okay. Here, let me get you some water before you go."

He shrieked again.

"Shh!" To my surprise, he stopped.

I stepped backward. Rabbits didn't speak English. They did pick up on emotions, though, so maybe he caught my stress when he screamed. I refilled the water bottle on the side of the hutch, then leaned against the counter, sipping my own glass while I waited for Kevin to come back downstairs.

"How is he?" I asked when my brother returned, pointing at the ceiling.

"Fine. He said something woke him up. I gave him hugs and

we said our ABCs and he went right back to sleep." Kevin gestured at the cage. "What about that one?"

"I'm not entirely sure. Seems stressed but physically okay. What happened?"

"No clue. He appeared to be fine. When I undid the deadbolt, he started screaming. I started to take him into the garage so he wouldn't wake Kyle, but as soon as I opened the door, he launched himself at the sides of the cage. I set him on the table to calm him."

"It seemed to have worked." The rabbit now lay curled up on the bottom of his cage, apparently asleep.

"Great. Now that my heart rate is back to normal, I'd like to go see my girlfriend." Kevin stepped toward the cage. Instantly, the bunny bolted upright and glared at him. "What's going on?"

"Um, this is going to sound weird, but I think he wants to stay here," I said.

The bunny clucked.

Kevin looked from me to the cage and back a few times. "Let's try an experiment." He stepped toward the cage. The bunny hissed. He stepped back. "Your turn."

I stepped toward the cage. The bunny clucked again. I shrugged and raised my hands. "What can I say? I have a way with small children and animals."

"We should call you Sofia the First."

I grinned at him. "I will happily move into a castle if you insist. Now go. Julie's going to worry about you."

"I'll call her from the car," he said as he opened the garage door. "Oh, and Aly?"

"Yeah?"

"I don't want you confronting Mary and Priscilla yourself. This is a matter for the authorities."

"Oh, I won't," I assured him. I might know a little self-defense, but taking on a suspected murderer myself? No, thank you.

After an extremely eventful day, I didn't really feel like banging my head against the wall… Er, doing research. But my inability to call up a vision was increasingly frustrating, and I needed to know what went wrong.

The first article I found was about a woman who sued a hospital for six hundred thousand dollars because a CAT scan made her lose her psychic powers. Having not been to a hospital recently, I discounted that one pretty quickly.

After about an hour of reading, I discovered a few competing theories. One, a person with magical powers could lose them if they didn't use their abilities for the greater good. That went along with what Mom had told me. But at the same time, I'd been trying to do just that when I'd discovered my powers went missing. Unless someone didn't want me to help Rusty, that didn't make sense. It's not like we were cheating on the investigator's exam or something.

Another site suggested that two psychics could act as dampers on each other's powers when they spent too much time in close proximity. There were as many articles debunking that theory as supporting it. Since Kevin and I lived together when I first found out about my powers, and both of us had been fine for the last eleven months, that didn't seem likely, either. I bookmarked a couple of files for later, but that theory felt like a dead end.

Option three: I'd been overtaxing myself, overusing my powers, stressing myself out too much. Blah. Summer school courses were intense, with three months' worth of information collapsed into six weeks. Finals caused stress, and my exam was next Tuesday. But if I needed to rest, fine. For Jeff's sake, I hoped one good night's sleep would be enough.

Time to switch gears. Priscilla and Mary were out there, and as far as I knew, whatever made them want Kyle in the first place hadn't gone away.

When we met, Mary gave me a cursed rocking chair that was intended for my nephew. Who knew what would have happened if Olive hadn't discovered the booby trap first? She'd been knocked out and it took more than a day for her to recover her powers. There was no way of knowing how the curse might have affected a small child.

I shivered at the thought. Those aunties would get my nephew over my dead body. Someone needed to stop them. Really, I should find out if they had some kind of magical police for witchy crimes. If not, what was I going to do? Call the local sheriff and tell him that he needed to lock up Mary for magical assault? Let them know I scried a magical vision of Priscilla killing Katrina?

None of that mattered if I couldn't find the Towne cousins and figure out what they were up to. To start, I pulled up the email address I'd created for this purpose. Personally, I'd rather text, but people my brother's age tended to have email. It had been a few days since I checked it, so it took a minute to scroll through the list.

Ad.

Ad.

Male performance enhancements ad.

Wait. There! Something caught my eye, and I stopped a split second before hitting "delete all." Mallory Weisberger had sent me a message. My heart lodged in my throat. According to Katrina's friend Christie, Mallory had been scheduled to act as a bridesmaid in Kevin and Katrina's wedding. At the last moment, she'd broken her leg in a skiing accident. My brother confirmed all that when I'd asked him. As much as he didn't want me poking around his wife's death, he'd finally realized he wasn't going to stop me.

Katrina and I hadn't been close, but anyone could see how her death affected him. Sure, he'd started dating Julie, but it took a long time and he still hadn't told Kyle. It killed me that Kyle would grow up never knowing what happened to his mother. They both deserved peace. I wanted to be the one to give it to them.

Hardly daring to breathe, I clicked on the message. It was short and to the point, without even a basic greeting at the beginning.

Christie is such a sweetie, glad you got to meet her. All of us were so bummed when I broke my leg right before the wedding. Luckily, Priscilla was free to take my place. Le sigh, there's not much else I can tell you. Much love to Kevin. Everyone misses him.

That was it. I read the message three times, not wanting to believe I'd spent months trying to get in touch with this woman for a six-sentence message. A weird-sounding one at that. Le sigh? What did that even mean?

Hold on a sec.

Who were "all of us" and "everyone"? Katrina had five bridesmaids. Two of them were Priscilla and Mary. Naomi was an exchange student who moved back to Japan like ten years ago. So... Christie missed my brother? She hadn't said so when Sam and I met her. She also said she wasn't in contact with Mallory.

I read the message again, unable to shake the sense I was missing something. Why was the message unsigned? Sure, Mallory's name showed in the header but most people still did a greeting and/or sign off when messaging a total stranger. "Christie is such a sweetie" was such a weird salutation. Had my message looked so weird?

I scrolled down, but no, it was just a basic "Hey, I'd love to chat!" message. Didn't say much. I did pose several questions to her, such as "Did Priscilla and/or Mary seem like they were acting odd before the wedding?" and "Did you by any chance get the same tattoo as the others?" She hadn't bothered to address any of it. Just a bunch of weirdness.

Le sigh.

Much love.

Hold on.

Back to the top I went. Then I looked at each sentence again. Sure, I'd never met Mallory, but the language didn't flow right. Something was off. Maybe she wasn't a native English speaker? But still. Quickly, I opened a blank word processor page and pasted the message. Maybe I was trying too hard to read something into this, but all of my senses were on high alert.

I'd learned months ago to listen when the universe spoke to me. Why did she ignore all my questions? What was she trying to say?

Maybe it would make more sense if I broke the sentences up.

Christie is such a sweetie, glad you got to meet her.
All of us were so bummed when I broke my leg right before the
wedding.
Luckily, Priscilla was free to take my place.
Le sigh, there's not much else I can tell you.
Much love to Kevin.
Everyone misses him.

And there it was, down the left side of the page.

CALLME.

My whole body tingled. Mallory knew something. Something big enough that she didn't want to risk putting it in writing.

CHAPTER ELEVEN

ABOUT FOUR SECONDS after cracking the code from Mallory's email, my elation evaporated. How could I call without her phone number? Including it in the message might have been helpful. No less weird than everything else she said.

There were three possibilities: one, I was having delusions of grandeur. Seeing myself as a code breaker on top of psychic, bunny saver, super aunt, and straight-A biology major. Two, Mallory was smart enough to think of a code but not to tell me how to get in touch with her. That seemed unlikely. Three, she'd send me another coded message with the actual number.

To start, I typed Mallory's name into the search bar, but only one message came up. Naturally, it wasn't that easy. The letters CALLME couldn't possibly create a number when typed into a phone—and even if they did, I wasn't prepared to accept that big of a coincidence. Then I went to Facebook and punched in her name to see if she had magically created an account since the last time I checked. A big fat "nope" there. Back to the inbox.

Mentally, I reviewed the information at hand. Mallory and Katrina had been best friends before the wedding, and there wasn't any reason to think the broken leg ended their friendship. What happened to Katrina's phone when she died? Maybe I already had the number, if it hadn't changed.

After getting married, Kevin and Katrina had moved to the 'burbs. Bought the huge, fancy house, Kevin went to work a zillion hours a week. They had a baby and started their perfect life. White picket fence and all. When she died, my brother shut down. He hadn't been able to stand looking at her things, so he'd put most of it into storage before moving to Shady Grove. Last spring, I'd gone with Sam to dig through the unit. I didn't remember seeing her phone.

It wasn't something we'd been looking for, but since we'd been hoping to find evidence of who killed her, it seemed like I would have kept her phone if we'd stumbled across it. I could call Sam to ask if he remembered it, but I didn't want to interrupt his studying when it seemed a total long shot. Was Katrina's old phone in Kevin's bedroom?

Nah, I'd searched pretty thoroughly last spring, looking for clues. I could look again, especially since he wouldn't be coming home until early morning, but it seemed like a waste of time.

As I was sitting there, trying to figure out the next step, my tablet pinged with another new message notification.

In my inbox, I spotted the thing I'd been looking for: a second message from Mallory. Either she realized I had no way of actually calling, or she'd wanted to break up the emails in case someone was reading them. Paranoid, or a wise precaution? Under the circumstances, any step that might protect Kyle made me feel better about the person exercising it.

With a deep breath, I clicked to open the email.

Aly,

By the way, I remember your brother telling me you liked science. Me, too! When I lived in Boston, my favorite elements were boron and cesium. I'm also partial to sodium and potassium.

- Mallory

Sodium and potassium? Those elements exploded when mixed together. Was Mallory threatening me? But what about the boron and cesium? I was all in favor of having favorite elements (selenium), but extensive research told me I was virtually alone in this. Except for my friend Tiffaneigh (carbon, because it made diamonds when under pressure). But... no, wait.

The first message was in code. This one was too weird not to be the same. Boron was element number five. Cesium was element fifty-five. And 555 was a phone number exchange. Add atomic numbers eleven (sodium) and nineteen (potassium) and all of a sudden, I was looking at a seven-digit telephone number.

Since Mallory hadn't lived in Boston when Katrina and Kevin got married, I assumed that comment was to direct me to her current area code. If she had a cell phone, technically the number could have been from anywhere—but why mention geography if it wasn't for a purpose? I could be wrong, but according to the internet, Boston only had two area codes. It would take three seconds to try them both.

Biting my lip, I glanced at the clock. It was almost nine o'clock, but that second email came through less than five minutes ago.

This had to work. These messages were coded for a reason. You didn't need to be psychic to know something was off, and I happened to *be* psychic. Not about things like this, but still. Time to find out what Mallory knew.

Fingers crossed, I switched to my calling app and dialed, starting with 617 because it came up first on Google.

A woman answered my call so quickly, I didn't even hear it ringing on my end. Her voice was metallic, scratchy. Like she used something to disguise it. This woman wasn't taking any chances. I couldn't decide whether that was terrifying or comforting. It was definitely weird.

"Aly," she said. "That was fast. I'm impressed you figured it out so easily."

"How did you know it was me?" I asked.

"Only a few people have this number," she said. "I guess you know who I am."

"A fan of exploding potassium?"

Her amusement traveled clearly down the line. "Something like that."

As badly as I wanted to cut to the chase, something was bugging me. "How did you know I'm familiar with the periodic table?"

"You're named after one of the elements. Your brother was named after a scientific measurement. It seemed like a logical conclusion. If you hadn't called, I'd have come up with a Plan B."

"Kevin changed his name when he was eighteen. Why would he tell you about it?"

"To be honest, he probably wouldn't have, but remember— we met in college. Lots of frat parties. The truth has a way of coming out at these things."

That rang somewhat true. Considering she'd responded directly to an email addressed to Mallory, I decided to give her the benefit of the doubt. "You know Mary Towne and Priscilla Huntington, right?"

"I used to. I knew Mary pretty well, because she and Katrina were BFFs when we met," Mallory said. "Priscilla had already moved to Baltimore. I didn't meet her until right before Kevin and Katrina's wedding."

"When she took your place as bridesmaid?"

"Right. I broke my leg, and fortunately we were the same size."

"I know this is going to sound completely out of left field, but can you tell me how you were injured?"

"Good question. I've played that day in my head dozens of times," Mallory said. "I grew up in Vermont, practically living on the slopes. My first job in high school was selling hot cocoa at the top of a ski lift. I learned to ski before I could walk."

"You fell?" I asked. "It's okay, it happens."

"True, but the weird thing was how I fell." Mallory lowered her voice. "Listen, Aly, what I'm going to tell you will sound unbelievable, and if you tell anyone, I'll deny it."

"A lot of formerly unbelievable things have happened to me over the past year," I said. "Chances are you can't tell me anything weirder than what I've already experienced."

She chuckled. "Touché. In that case—I think someone shoved me onto an icy patch so I would fall."

"I'm chasing a murderer. Why would that surprise me?"

"Because I was alone when it happened."

Most people probably would have had some sort of reaction to this news, but to me it made perfect sense. "Let me guess: did the other bridesmaids not wear the same size as Priscilla?"

"They did not," she confirmed. "But we were about the same height, with similar body types. Let me back up. Mary was worried about skiing. She said it was her first time since she'd been a little girl. Katrina wanted her to feel more comfortable, so I offered to take Mary up the lift and go down the bunny slopes. Naomi and Katrina went to try the intermediate slopes, and Christie decided to take a few black diamond runs on her own."

"Black diamond runs?" I grew up in a valley that never dropped below about thirty degrees. Skiing was as alien to me as Mars.

"That's the advanced slope," she said.

"Ah. Was that unusual? For Christie to leave the group?"

"Not really. She was a bit of an introvert, but also, she preferred snowboarding. She was dying to try some new tricks she'd seen on YouTube, and none of us saw a reason to delay her."

"Okay. So you were skiing with Mary, and you hit some ice?"

"Not exactly. Keep in mind, we were on the easiest part of a commercial ski slope. They're pretty good about making sure there's no ice where anyone could fall. Anyway, Mary and I went up the lift together. At the top, I gave her a pep talk, helped her get going, then hung back to make sure she was okay." I heard the sadness in her voice at the memory. "You know, I always thought we were friends."

"Did she come back and knock you over?"

"No, that's the weird thing. She definitely didn't. I adjusted my goggles and took off. About a third of the way down the slope, it was like my skis got a mind of their own. They turned toward the edge of the mountain, and I couldn't turn back. I tried to sit down to stop. That should have worked. It makes no sense that it didn't. But I couldn't sit. I couldn't stop. My skis took me off the trail, into the woods. Then they hit ice, and I skidded into a tree."

I gasped. "That sounds terrifying. I'm so sorry."

"Everyone said I fell, but that's not possible. I don't fall. I know it sounds unbelievable, but my skis were possessed. I think Mary did it. I don't know why, but I'd bet my life on it."

"What makes you say that?" The words may have suggested I didn't believe her, but hopefully my tone let her know we were on the same page.

Mallory took a deep breath. "Weird things happened around the Towne girls sometimes. All three of them. Things you couldn't explain, and they changed the subject if you asked. After a while, you learned not to say anything if you wanted to keep hanging out with them. Still, I never thought one of them would turn on me. Especially not Mary. She was so... milquetoast."

"She was like milky toast?"

"No, milquetoast. Bland, boring," she explained. "Priscilla hid it well, but she was the loose cannon."

Her words stirred something within me. The Mary and Priscilla I'd met recently had been almost exactly the opposite. Before that, I'd only seen them at the wedding. Where I was a gawky teenager, quiet, and not interesting at all to a couple of women in college. They barely spoke to me.

Mary was a witch, that I knew. Their grandmother had been descended from one of the victims of the Salem Witch Trials, and all the women in the family had powers. Whether that power included the ability to conjure a giant hand to push someone, I didn't know. No one had ever mentioned what Priscilla could or couldn't do, but she did sense my arrival at the rehab facility when I went to visit her earlier thi summer.

"There must have been some reason Mary wanted Priscilla to be in the wedding."

"If it was that important, they could have just told me," Mallory said.

"Agreed. Maybe they thought you wouldn't believe them, especially if it had to do with the weird things that sometimes happened around them."

"I guess."

The Priscilla I'd met at the rehab center told me that Mary had imprisoned her there against her will. When Kevin and I learned that Mary and Priscilla took off together, we'd thought she was a hostage. Now, it seemed more likely that the two of them were in cahoots.

I still didn't know which one of them killed Katrina. The scene I'd scried only showed me a woman about the same height as both cousins, with a tattoo I now knew they'd gotten at the same time. Hearing that Mary helped get Mallory out of the wedding party and Priscilla took her place made me wonder if they were working together.

Why would they kill their sister and cousin, though?

Mallory laughed nervously. "Have I sent you over the edge?"

I took a deep breath to clear my head. "I promise, I believe you. But do you really want to know what happened?"

"You know, I don't think it matters anymore. More than how I wonder why? Why would she do that?"

"That's the million-dollar question. To be honest, I was at the wedding, and I don't remember anything all that exciting happening. Nothing to explain why Priscilla would have needed to be a bridesmaid rather than a regular guest."

"It was a lovely ceremony."

"Hold on. You were there? I thought you couldn't go."

"I couldn't stand at the front for the whole thing in my cast, even with crutches. It felt weird, like everyone would be staring at me instead of Katrina." She paused. "It wouldn't have bothered her. I should have done it."

"There's no point second-guessing yourself now," I said. "Besides, what if you hadn't backed out and Priscilla had done something else?"

"That's a good point." Mallory's voice wavered. "Anyway, I have no idea what she wanted. Other than my dress. Which was really not worth committing conspiracy and assault for."

My lips twitched at the memory. My late sister-in-law generally had great taste, but bridesmaids' dresses had their own special magic—no one but the bride ever thought they looked good. "There are easier ways to get a dress than have your cousin attack someone."

"A fair point." She yawned loudly. "Listen, I'm sorry, but I have to go. It's been a long day."

"No problem. Thanks for your time." Suddenly, I remember one of the reasons I called. "Hey—did you get a tattoo?"

She paused. "Why do you ask?"

"Just curious," I said. "I don't have a lot of close friends, and I thought it was interesting that you all got matching ones."

"Yeah." She laughed. "It seemed like a good idea at the time. Sure, I got it. On the inside of my wrist. Every time I see it, I think of Katrina."

The words sent a shock through me. Mallory's tattoo was in the same location as the one I spotted on Katrina's killer in my vision. This whole time, I'd been pursuing Mary and Priscilla because they had the tattoo in the right spot. All of a sudden, a new suspect joined my list.

To fill the awkward silence, I said, "I miss her."

"I miss her, too," she said softly. "If I think of anything else, I'll let you know. Phone is better than email. This is a burner, so it's not linked to me. You never know who may be watching us."

Well, that was unsettling. I thanked her for the information, and we hung up. Her words played on repeat through my mind, but it still felt like I was missing a key element. Priscilla coordinated an attack on Mallory so she could be in Katrina's wedding—why? Mary helped her, again, why?

Then again—Mallory just told me she had the same tattoo in the same place. Was she so innocent she didn't know how incriminating that sounded? Or was she making herself seem trustworthy so I wouldn't suspect her?

CHAPTER TWELVE

THE NEXT MORNING, I spent ten minutes trying to conjure up a vision when I woke up, with no results. Granted, I owned most of the items in my bedroom, and I'd never had a vision starring myself, but still. I wasn't able to get a hint of Sam off his t-shirt I'd borrowed a couple of months ago or the ticket stubs from our first official date. Not even the ring I'd found in Missing Pieces, the item that originally triggered my psychic powers, told me anything

Whatever was affecting me yesterday hadn't gone away yet. I'd have to ask Olive about it.

The sounds of Kevin downstairs making breakfast lured me away from my tests. I was eager to talk to him about my conversation with Mallory before Kyle woke up. Once my nephew saw that his new bunny friend had followed me home, all chance for adult conversation would go out the window.

"Hey, big brother. How's Julie?" The coffee maker was on, so I grabbed a mug out of the cupboard. Kevin had showered and put on a fresh t-shirt, so he'd either been home a while or he took a change of clothes over there.

He grinned at me. The look on his face warmed my heart. It

had been too long since I saw him happy. "She's good. To what do I owe this pleasure?"

"Can't I get up early to have breakfast with my big brother?"

"You can, but in the year you've lived with us, I think that's happened twice. I can't remember the last time you woke up before Kyle."

"A fair point," I said. "I just wanted to talk to you before he came downstairs. I had an interesting conversation with one of Katrina's old friends last night."

After pouring myself a mug of coffee, I slathered some hazelnut spread on two pieces of toast and settled into the chair across from Kevin.

"Is Priscilla a witch?" I asked over a delicious mouthful. Preamble was for people with time to spare.

He snagged the second piece off my plate. I debated fighting him for it, but it was too early. He chewed thoughtfully for a moment before responding. "I don't think so. She had powers, like Katrina and Mary. But I always thought she was more like you."

"She had visions?"

"Sort of. She got feelings," he said. "Like, one time, she had a strong sense Katrina shouldn't take the subway home. We argued about it, because college students don't have a lot of extra money for taxis, and it was too far to walk. Ten minutes later, she gave in abruptly, and we headed for the subway."

"She had a feeling about nothing?"

"The train ahead of us jumped the track. Four people were injured."

Oh, wow. That revelation rocked me back in my seat, so stunned I almost dropped my coffee. With a shaking hand, I set it on the table.

When I'd gone to visit Priscilla at Destiny's Haven, she'd somehow known that I was going to show up, although no one could have told her. If she had visions of the future, that explained a lot. Maybe she'd needed to be a bridesmaid to prevent something from happening?

I didn't recall anything out of the ordinary at Kevin and Katrina's wedding, but I'd been a teenager. The time not spent with my parents helping with last-minute preparations and planning mostly went to reading so I didn't fall behind on my schoolwork (yes, I was a nerd in high school, too) or texting my friends.

"Was there any sort of incident at your wedding?" I asked. "Did Priscilla or Mary save the day or anything like that?"

"That's a weird question," Kevin said.

"Mallory thinks Mary made her fall so Priscilla could take her place," I explained. "With magic. I didn't know why Mary would care so much about her cousin being a bridesmaid, but if Priscilla had a vision…?"

He thought for a long time. "I don't remember. I'm sorry. That probably means nothing major, but I'll think about it."

"Do you have a copy of the wedding video here? Or is it in the—" I cut myself off with a coughing fit. Kevin didn't know I knew about his storage unit down by the city. Or at least he hadn't until three seconds ago.

"Aly? Is there anything you want to tell me?" Kevin asked.

"Nope." Not a lie. I did not want to tell him I riffled through all his stuff while claiming to be on a date with Sam.

That technically wasn't a lie, either. The whole thing was oddly date-like. We held hands, and we shared some smooches.

"You know I can get it out of you, right?"

"Dear Brother, I think this is one thing you'd prefer I not elaborate on. Back to my original question. Do you have a video from the wedding here? I'd like to watch and see if anything out of the ordinary happened."

"Sorry, no. It's in my top-secret and extremely private storage unit that you very clearly know about." He gazed at me steadily for a long moment before draining his coffee and setting his mug on the table. "If I'm not mistaken, I hear a little boy moving around upstairs. A little boy who is about to have a very exciting morning."

"Daddy! I need underwear!" Kyle's voice carried clearly down the stairs. He'd been delayed a bit after his mother's death, and while his speech was finally catching up to his peers, we hadn't quite gotten up the nerve to tackle nighttime potty training.

I laughed. "Remind me why Julie doesn't want to sleep over here?"

My brother's face turned bright red. "Shh!"

Before I forgot, I texted Sam to ask if he had time to go with me to Kevin's storage unit to search for the wedding video before school started. I really wanted to see it.

Resisting the urge to roll my eyes, I pointed at the stairs. "You're up."

A moment later, the thud thud of little feet propelled Kyle down the stairs. I knew the second he spotted the small gray and white rabbit in his hutch on the coffee table. That little boy's squeal of delight would have reached my ears on Mars.

"Bunny! Daddy, I want to play with the bunny."

Pulling myself to my feet, I went to the living room doorway. Kyle stood in his blue and red superhero pajamas, bouncing up and down. Kevin waited on the staircase, watching his son with a mixture of love and amusement.

With exaggerated movements, I dropped my mouth open and brought both hands to my cheeks. "Oh my goodness! When did you get a bunny?"

"I don't know!"

I struggled to hide the enormous grin threatening to break across my face. "I believe this little guy is hungry. I hear that the best person to feed a rabbit is a little boy. Do you know any almost-four-year old boys who live around here?"

"Me! I'm almost four!"

Over his head, my brother glared at me. Then, his eyes

brightened as if he'd had a brainstorm. "What do you want to name the bunny?"

My nephew looked from the cage to me to Kevin and back before yelling, "Daddy!"

"You want to name the bunny 'Daddy'?" I asked. "I think that name might be taken."

My brother shrugged. "It beats Kelvy."

"Kelvy!" Kyle yelled.

I didn't bother to conceal my snort of laughter.

Kevin coughed. "I walked into that one. Listen, Little Man, this rabbit is only staying with us until we find its owner. When I said you could get a pet, I meant a fish. Right, Aly?"

"The bunny is going away?" Kyle asked. He looked so sad, I wanted to promise him everything in the world to make that tiny frown go away.

Which was precisely why I didn't get to make the big decisions.

I tousled Kyle's hair. "Remember, this bunny wasn't for sale. We need to give him back to his owner."

"Speaking of the owner," Kevin said loudly. "Have you had any luck getting in touch with him?"

I shook my head, although to be fair I'd spent most of the prior evening doing research rather than looking for Jeff. But the local vet knew we'd taken the rabbit for safekeeping, not to mention Olive. Plus, I'd left a note *and* sent an email. Surely if Jeff returned to the store or his home last night, he would have texted me.

My stomach dropped as realization sank in. No word from Jeff meant he was still missing. Sure, Tory didn't seem at all concerned about her brother, but Dr. Younger's words kept coming back to me. Jeff was excited to be starting his own business. He loved his animals. That didn't sound like someone who would run away—even if he owed people money.

I'd helped police investigate a few murders since moving to Shady Grove. Never had there been the possibility of finding the person alive. I wanted to solve this mystery so badly, I could taste it.

Who could have a motive to hurt Jeff? Rainbow, obviously, although she didn't seem strong enough to drag a grown man away against his will. Maybe he'd been unconscious? Or maybe she'd had help. I couldn't dismiss her yet. Tory didn't seem happy that her brother kept asking for money or remotely concerned he was gone. Had she decided to permanently stop him from talking to her husband?

Then there was TJ. I didn't trust him. He'd been in the pet shop after the earthquake. He didn't ask where Jeff was or if there was an employee around, despite knowing I didn't work at the pet store. Maybe he knew Jeff wouldn't be there? He'd also promised to call the police but didn't.

Back to Rainbow. If she had a regular nail salon, I'd make an appointment and go on in. But a regular nail salon couldn't drive me out to the middle of nowhere and drop my dead body off a mountain. My whole life, I'd been told to avoid getting into a van with strangers.

Instead, I texted Rusty. He'd go with me to the murder van.

Er… The manicurist on wheels.

Once I got him to agree, I dug out the business card Rainbow had given me and called the number to set up our appointments. Her first opening was at one o'clock, and she assured me she could fit me and Rusty in at the same time. Hopefully not for a double homicide.

This seemed like a bad idea. I reminded myself repeatedly that Rainbow appeared to be about sixty years old and weigh barely one hundred pounds. If necessary, Rusty could sit on her while I drove to safety.

It would be fine. Everything would be fine.

Kevin sent Kyle to get our copy of the local paper off the front porch. "What are you doing?"

"It's time for work. Then Rusty and I are going to get pedi-cures," I said.

"What about your final?"

"It's only an elective. I can study tonight." I glanced at the clock. "Will you be home for dinner?"

"Sure," he replied distractedly as Kyle returned with the newspaper.

I said my goodbyes and gave my nephew both hugs and kisses before heading for the garage door.

"Hey, Aly!" Kevin's tone stopped me in my tracks. "Come back for a second."

"Sure. What's up?" I walked back to the kitchen doorway and cocked my head, prepared for another warning to be careful or mind my own business.

Instead, Kevin held up a copy of the *Shady Grove Sentinel* in both hands, letting it unfold. His face was white.

The photograph on the main page showed the exterior of the pet store, with me and Kyle standing outside. His face was blurred, at least. The image of me wasn't terribly flattering, but that wasn't the upsetting part. The headline leaped off the page.

PAWS AND EFFECT? WHEN LOCAL COLLEGE GIRL ARRIVES, CHAOS ENSUES.

CHAPTER THIRTEEN

A GROAN SLIPPED OUT, and I sank onto a stool beside the island. Kevin moved closer, eyes scanning the words frantically. "Do you want me to read the article to you?"

Covering my face with my hands, I shook my head. "Please just tell me it doesn't mention my powers anywhere."

"Not that I can see. Mostly he's commenting on your impressive detective skills in a way that makes people wonder if you've been killing people and framing others so you could 'solve' the crimes to make yourself look good."

I snorted. Of all the times I'd complained there wasn't anything to do in Shady Grove, that one never occurred to me. "Does he actually call me a murderer?"

"Of course not. Then you could sue." Kevin folded the paper and dropped it onto the counter. "It's all garbage. No one with any sense would believe a word of it, but I can demand he print a retraction."

People with sense didn't bother me. The Sheriff of Shady Grove bothered me. We had a county sheriff without much of a county, and not even ten thousand people to keep track of. He didn't have enough to do to keep him busy, and the last thing I needed was for him to decide to figure out how to tie me to a bunch of crimes. Especially when he was still mad about that time I proved he'd wrongfully arrested Olive.

"How is this front-page news?"

Kevin flipped the paper over. "Page two is about Amira's lost dog."

Right. In a small town, anything was big news. "Does it say how she found him?"

He scanned the page. "It says 'after hearing barking from inside her neighbor's garage,' she called Mr. Chang."

Thank goodness for small favors. "What about the earthquake? That matters."

His forehead wrinkled as he scanned the pages. "It's here, under the fold. You beat it."

"Yay?" I had so many better things to worry about, but I couldn't just let it go. "I need to go to the Sentinel's office."

"Why? Are you going to confront this guy?"

"Shouldn't I? If I don't talk to him, he might keep printing garbage about me."

"I put garbage in the trash can," Kyle said proudly, reminding me of his presence.

"Good job!" Kevin gave his son a high-five before turning back to me. "Or he might write that you threatened him. It's sometimes better to let these things blow over."

A heavy sigh escaped my lips. "There's nothing I can do?"

"You could have your devastatingly handsome and brilliant lawyer brother send them a letter demanding a retraction," Kevin said. "I'll only charge you half my normal fee."

"I hope your normal fee is about ten bucks, then."

"You can work it off in babysitting," he said.

"You don't pay me to babysit."

"I let you live here. Don't you have to get to work?"

"Ack! Sorry. And thank you! You're the best brother ever."

"Take the bunny with you!" he called after me.

Argh. I almost made it. I stopped and stuck my tongue out

at him. Then I picked up the rabbit cage. "Come on, Kelvy. Let's go find your owner."

Before my brother could tell me to stay out of the investigation, I raced toward my car.

For once, I managed to find a parking space directly in front of the store. I got to Missing Pieces right on time, but not early enough to talk to Olive about my glitchy powers.

About an hour after I arrived, things finally started to slow down. I was preparing to broach the subject when a man who looked around forty-five entered the store. I'd seen him around town and thought he worked at Patti's Diner, but didn't know his name.

"Good morning!" I said. "Welcome to Missing Pieces. Can I help you find something?"

"Thanks, but I don't think so." He brushed a wet gray curl out of his face. "It started to rain, and I had a feeling I should come in to wait out the storm."

"Well, you're in the right place! We've got a treasure trove, just waiting for you to find the piece that's missing from your life." I'd been practicing lines that tied into the store's name for a few months now. It passed the time on slow days.

Olive appeared in the door separating our main sales floor from the back. "Hello! I have just the thing for you."

After a moment, she stood up, tapping one finger to her mouth. She turned and walked toward the jewelry section. The man looked at me uncertainly. "Should I go with her? I wasn't looking for jewelry."

"Olive has a knack for helping people find things they didn't know they wanted," I said. "The storm's not going to let up for a bit. Go with her."

"Okay." He trailed behind Olive, out of sight. A moment later, their voices carried to me, but not clearly enough to hear the words. Since they wouldn't need my help, I turned back to the printout on the counter.

A few minutes later, Olive walked past, the man trailing

behind her like a lost lamb. They went into the housewares section. Huh. Usually Olive knew in advance when someone was coming for a particular object. She rarely gave customers a tour of the store before leading them to the right item.

Ah, well. Maybe the customer wanted more than one thing. Plenty of people loved antiques and stocked up while they were here. Back to the books.

A loud crash took me away from my task and around the counter toward the sound. "Olive!"

"I'm okay," she called back. "Dan's got me."

When I walked around the stacks, the man who must be Dan was helping Olive to her feet as she shook her head. A pile of glass sat at her feet. "I'm sorry, I don't know what's come over me."

"Are you hurt?" I asked. "What happened?"

"She dropped a vase," Dan said. "Too bad. It was nice."

"I'm okay," Olive said. "But I think I might be coming down with something."

Dan dropped Olive's hand like a hot potato. "Germs? You're sick? I'm sorry, I have to go. Look, the rain is letting up after all."

"No, wait! It's not that kind of sick," I started.

It was too late. The bells jingled merrily as the door swung shut behind him. He didn't even stop to say goodbye. Weird.

As soon as the door shut, I whirled around to face my boss. She stared at the door with a bemused expression. "What's wrong, Olive?"

"What are you talking about?" Her feigned innocence was even less believable than Kyle's.

"Come on. I've seen you unite dozens of people with their 'missing pieces', and never once have I seen you look like you were smelling sulfur while you did it. Was something wrong with that vase?"

"No." She paused, patting her hair. "Yes, maybe. I don't know."

Taking her by the arm, I led her to the small bistro set that remained perpetually for sale by the cash register. Well, theoretically for sale but in reality a nice resting place. The fact that she didn't resist shook me almost as much as her demeanor working with Dan.

"Don't move," I said once she was seated.

In the back room, we had a coffee maker and electric tea kettle. While normally coffee was my drink of choice, this felt like a tea-drinking moment. I started the kettle and leaned against the counter to steady myself.

Element sixteen was sulfur. Element seventeen was chlorine. That kind of rhymed. Element eighteen was argon, which didn't rhyme at all. Time to grab a broom and dustpan.

By the time I finished sweeping up the broken shards of vase, the kettle had started whistling. It only took a moment to prepare the tea tray Olive kept in the back and carry it to the front room.

When she sipped from her cup, some of the color finally returned to my boss's face. "Thank you."

"You're welcome," I said, dropping into the chair beside her. "Now are you ready to tell me what's going on?"

"To be honest, I'm not sure," she said. "I know that vase belonged to Dan because I saw him the other morning when it arrived. I was expecting him. But when I picked it up just now, it didn't speak to me at all."

"Isn't that normal? You already know who it belongs to."

"True, but my powers don't fade until an object is placed with the right person. I should be able to pick it up at any time and see the owner's face."

Huh.

"What are you saying, Olive?"

"Something's happened to me. My power is gone."

CHAPTER FOURTEEN

OLIVE LOST HER ABILITIES, too. I hadn't had a vision since yesterday morning. How was that possible? For a full thirty seconds after she dropped her bomb, I just stared at her with my mouth open.

Finally, I said, "Me, too."

"Really? That's astounding." She sounded as dumbfounded as if I'd started reeling off the radioactive elements.

"Both of us. Can that happen?"

"I wouldn't have thought so, but it did."

"Are you sick?" I asked. "I'm tired but otherwise okay."

She shook her head. "Other than this, I feel great. How long has this been going on?"

"At least since yesterday," I admitted. "I kept trying to induce visions off electronics, and that's spotty on a good day. Plus, the bunny thing. I never expected to get a vision from handling an animal. But it seemed odd that nothing in the pet store or Jeff's house sparked anything."

"You went inside Jeff's house?" I opened my mouth, but she put her hand up. "Never mind. I don't want to know. When was the last time you had a vision?"

I thought about that for a long time. "Friday morning. Rusty brought me a woman's scarf to find out if she was cheating on her husband."

"So that's what? More than forty-eight hours without a vision."

"Yeah. I don't have them every day, but something is definitely wrong." I said. "What do we do?"

"I'll do some research," Olive said. "See if there's anything in the air at the shop that might have caused this. We got a shipment on Wednesday evening. Maybe some chemical on the cardboard boxes?"

"When did you last use your powers?"

She thought for a minute. "I'm not certain. I got the feeling about Dan's vase earlier this week, but it could have been Wednesday or Thursday morning."

"Try to remember?"

"Oh, now the student has become the teacher?" She winked at me, then made a shooing motion. "You should get out of here. If your power loss has to do with this store, you need to go somewhere else."

"I'm not leaving you alone."

"I was alone for twenty years before you came along."

"And isn't that sad?" Her lips twitched with amusement, so I continued. "Listen. Call Amira to see if she has any suggestions. I'll go next door and get us some coffee. You want a Julie special?"

She nodded. Olive liked to try new things, and Julie enjoyed trying out weird new recipes on her. The weirder, the better. The two of them made quite a pair.

Next door, Julie stood behind the counter of On What Grounds?, as usual. She'd had a string of managers since Rusty left, none of whom worked out. Most days, she claimed to blame me, but she was kidding.

Hopefully.

To my surprise when I entered the coffee shop, Kevin stood behind the counter wearing an apron. After a rather memorable

Christmas vacation during college, he'd sworn never to work in food service again. The fact that he'd break his vow to help Julie made me smile.

I approached the counter and gave my order. "The legal business not as fulfilling as you'd hoped, Kev?"

His cheeks turned pink. "My first meeting today isn't until eleven. I thought I'd help out for a bit."

"Well, the uniform suits you." Julie suited him.

"Thanks. What are you up to?"

"Olive and I have some stuff to do, and I'm still trying to find Jeff so I can return his rabbit and stop making my brother hate me."

"I don't hate—Hold on. What was that?"

Oops. We co-existed better when he pretended not to know I wasn't doing things he disapproved of. "Get the rabbit out of my brother's house?"

"Aly, you swore you weren't going to get involved with this," Kevin said sternly.

I glanced around, but other than the three of us, the shop was empty.

"Yes, but you knew I was lying."

"That's—" He broke off, staring at me intently. "No, I didn't."

Uh-oh. I didn't like where this was headed. "What are you talking about? Yes, you did. It's one of your most annoying qualities."

"I'm sure you meant 'most lovable'," he said. "But no. I actually felt comforted when I went to Julie's last night because you'd said you were going to leave this to the professionals, and I believed you. Have you become immune to my powers?"

I shrugged. "I hate superhero movies."

Julie snorted. "Even I know that's a lie."

"It is, but I can't *see it*," Kevin said. "Have your powers gotten stronger?"

"Maybe? I mean, I would hope so. I spend a lot of time practicing. But honestly, I don't think my powers would let me lie better."

"Are you taking any drama electives at school?" Julie asked.

"I wish." I sighed, then a thought hit me. "Hold on. Julie, lie to me."

"What? Why?" Realization slowly dawned. "You want to know if it's everyone or just you."

"Exactly."

She turned toward my brother. "Okay, I'm going to tell you two truths and a lie."

"I love this game!" They both looked at me, and my cheeks grew warm. "Sorry, not the point."

Julie thought for a minute. "Got it. Number one, I prefer hot cocoa to coffee. Number two, I like the way the subway smells. Number three, I've never been married."

I wrinkled my nose. "No one likes the smell on the subway."

"Don't help," Kevin said. "I know number one is true. But if I'm relying solely on my powers, it's all three. I don't see anything."

Julie shook her head. "I actually do like the smell on the subway. Sure, it's gross, but it's also got that unique New York City vibe to it. It smells like home."

"You've been married?" Kevin asked.

She averted her eyes and took a big swig of coffee. "Maybe I should have found another way to bring that up. But I figured it wasn't a big deal since you—"

"Guys!" They both jumped, somehow having forgotten I was there. "This is super important and you should definitely talk about it later, but at the moment, we have bigger fish to fry. Kevin, has this ever happened to you before?"

"Not that I know of. I wouldn't necessarily know if a stranger lied to me, but since my twenty-first birthday, I've seen lies pretty frequently. Nothing the past day or so."

"And you didn't notice?"

"Sorry, I was distracted by my baby sister's new pet rabbit."

I shot him a withering look. "Try to focus."

Olive's psychic ability was gone. In the past twenty-four hours or so, I hadn't induced a single vision. Kevin couldn't see my lies. That couldn't be a coincidence.

Something was happening to the residents of Shady Grove. Something took our powers.

"You look like someone just told you carbon isn't really an element," Kevin said. "I'm probably coming down with something."

"I don't think so. It's not just you," I said.

"You, too?"

"And Olive."

"Wow. Okay. Wow," Julie said.

"My thoughts exactly," Kevin said.

"Right there with you," I said. "So what do we do?"

Kevin said, "Let's think this through. You're a scientist. Or you will be. What do scientists do when facing a problem?"

"Form a hypothesis, do tests," I recite automatically.

"Exactly. What's your hypothesis here?"

"It has to be the bunny." I felt silly just saying it. "How else do you explain the fact that our powers have vanished just when this thing came into our lives?"

"Because finding the bunny isn't the only unusual thing to happen recently, and the other one was a seismic event of the type that never occurs in this part of the country."

The earthquake.

No, Kyle had his powers after the earthquake. When we'd run into Amira outside the pet store, he'd immediately told her where to find her missing dog. If all the magical people were losing their powers, whatever happened must've been after that.

It had to be the bunny.

Oh, fluorine.

With effort, I swallowed a groan of frustration. Kevin never wanted me to bring that rabbit into our house in the first place.

He'd tried to leave with it, to get it away from me and Kyle. The "I-told-you-so" that was coming would be so glorious, so heartfelt, it would put all other "I-told-you-so"s in the history of conversation to shame.

He didn't say anything, and I wondered if he was mentally reciting the elements of the periodic table until he was calm enough not to throttle me. I closed my eyes, bracing for the onslaught of words.

It never came.

After a moment, I felt a cool touch on my arm. Julie. "It's okay, Aly. You didn't know."

I cracked one eye to look at my brother. "Does he see it that way?"

"I probably will when I calm down," Kevin said. "But what atrocious timing. Here I am, doing everything I can to find Mary and Priscilla—"

"Excuse me?" I put my hands on my hips. "Whatever happened to 'stay out of it'? To 'let the professionals handle this?'"

His cheeks turned red. "That's what I tell my baby sister. It doesn't apply to me."

"I'm not a kid anymore, Kevin! I've helped solve three murders."

"And I will never forgive myself for putting you in harm's way like that. If you hadn't moved to Shady Grove, you never would have had to deal with any of this."

At the edge of my vision, Julie backed away slowly, slinking behind the counter and toward the swinging kitchen door. A wise woman. I didn't want to be part of this conversation, either. "I love Shady Grove, Kev. I love my job and my classes and you and Kyle and Olive and I love my—" I broke off at the words that almost came out of my mouth, the revelation that I'd fallen in love with Sam. No big surprise, surely, but also the kind of thing you wanted to share with your boyfriend before telling your big brother. "—life."

Even without his powers, after living together all this time, Kevin saw right through me. "Life, huh? Is that what you call Sam when the two of you are alone?"

I bit back a retort and shook my head. "What are we dealing with here? A magic bunny? Are magic bunnies a thing?"

From the kitchen door, a voice shouted, "Are psychics a thing? Witches?"

Kevin chuckled. "She's got a point."

"Fair enough," I said. "But how? Why? And how are we supposed to figure this out? It's not like I can ask the bunny."

"Have you tried?" Kevin asked.

"You're asking me if I've tried having a conversation with the magic bunny?" I spoke very slowly. "Julie, what's in these baked goods?"

She snorted and came back into the front of the store. "Since it's no use pretending I'm not listening, I might as well stand where I can hear you. Does anyone else want more coffee?"

Kevin and I moved out of the way while Julie fired up the espresso machine.

"Should I go get Kelvy from Olive so we can figure this out?" I asked.

Kevin shook his head. "Not yet. I'm not sure we want the bunny to know we're on to him."

I fought to keep a straight face. "It's not funny!"

"No, it really is," he said. "But it's also serious. Is this a temporary problem or permanent? Is he stealing our powers or draining them? For what purpose? Is the whole thing a giant coincidence?"

I thought quickly while Julie brought our drinks to the table. A long swallow of steaming vanilla latte always cleared my head. "The first step is to form a hypothesis, right? You said it yourself. That's what Rusty and I did when I first started having visions."

"Of course it is. That's so you."

Ignoring the comment, I said, "We hypothesize that this

rabbit from the pet shop somehow caused us to lose our powers. If we could find Jeff—"

"Who?" Julie interjected.

"The pet store owner," I said. "Which makes him this rabbit's owner."

"Right, okay." She thought for a moment. "Are any of the other animals magic?"

That was an excellent question, and of course no one knew the answer. All we had were more questions. I shrugged helplessly, because really, how did you even begin to test that one?

"Let's deal with one thing at a time," I said. "Missing powers first. Our hypothesis is that the rabbit, what, took them?"

"Or somehow affects them," Kevin said. "But to what extent? You haven't had any visions since picking him up, right?"

"Yeah. I tried to inspire one in the pet store, but it didn't work."

Julie asked, "That didn't make you suspicious?"

I gave her a wry smile. "Unfortunately, about half the time, my attempts fail. I'm still learning. But I've been trying to figure this out on my own."

She nodded and patted my hand, then picked up her mug.

"Is it only the three of us?" Kevin continued. "Or is it everyone who's had any interaction with him?"

"Not everyone." I looked at my brother meaningfully, thinking "Kyle" as loudly as I could.

He nodded. "Right. Does losing the magic require prolonged exposure? Does it go away if we move far enough away from him?"

All excellent questions. All questions I couldn't begin to answer. Except maybe that last one.

"Dear Brother," I said, "you've given me an idea. Let's find the limits of this thing."

"I better reschedule my appointment," Kevin said, picking up his phone.

Testing a hypothesis got me all tingly with excitement. The bunny was safe at Missing Pieces with Olive. Now that we knew he might be affecting her powers, we couldn't leave him there. But we could go pick him up and ask her to text the minute her powers returned. Assuming they did.

Oh, man. The thought that Olive might have lost her powers forever and it was all my fault made my face crumple. This was so unfair.

"Hey." Julie waved a hand in front of my face. "Whatever you're thinking, stop. We'll figure this out. Go get the bunny."

Kevin shot her a quizzical look. "You want him in the cafe?"

"Absolutely not. That's a health code violation. I'll take him upstairs to my place. I don't have any magical powers for him to suck away. You can pick him up later."

Like Olive, Julie lived in an apartment attached to the store. Unlike Olive, I suspected that Julie's apartment smelled like coffee and baked goods all the time. How a person could live above her coffee shop without being constantly starving was beyond me.

Speaking of starving, breakfast felt like a distant memory despite it being only a couple of hours ago. I stood up as my stomach rumbled loudly. "I'll go get Kelvy. But can you ring me up a muffin first? I need sugar and carbs for this."

She waved one hand. "This one's on me. In the name of science. What do you want?"

After Julie put a chocolate chip muffin for me and an apple croissant for Olive in a striped paper bag, I returned to Missing Pieces. It didn't take long to collect Kelvy and explain what was going on. Olive promised to let me know if she felt her powers return. If she didn't feel anything specific, she would test them hourly and let me know the results.

Meanwhile, since it wasn't as easy for me to call my powers on demand, Kevin would come with me while we moved away from Missing Pieces. I'd tell a lie, he'd let me know if he could see it.

This was going to be fun.

After my brother deposited the bunny in Julie's apartment, Kevin and I walked to the corner of Main Street and Second Street. I stopped and turned to face my brother. "Element number three is potassium."

"Is that a lie, or are you just wrong?"

"Shush," I told him. "What do you see?"

"An annoying little sister," he said. "Who is thinking about kicking me in the shins right now."

A bark of laughter escaped me. When we got to Town Square, I told another lie. "Nickelback is the greatest band of all time."

"You know you think that's true."

"Shush. What do you see?"

He sighed. "Nothing."

And so on. We walked back to our house, since we'd need a car to go much further. But how far were we supposed to go? What happened if Kevin still couldn't see lies when we drove ten miles away? A hundred? We couldn't spend all night driving to Montreal to solve a riddle that might not have an answer instead of studying.

But maybe I didn't have to. Maybe there was another way to test the limits of this thing.

"Come on. I've got an idea."

"Where are we going?"

"To see a friend."

CHAPTER FIFTEEN

TWENTY MINUTES LATER, we pulled into the circular driveway of an old house on the outskirts of town. During his life, the prior owner had lived in Shady Grove. He was considered a town fixture, like Thelma or Missing Pieces. Due to some zoning issue after he died, the house was now in Willow Falls. Personally, it didn't matter to me, except for the one key element: we weren't in Shady Grove anymore. Would we get our powers back now that we'd crossed the town line?

A sign out front welcomed us to *Emma's Home for Lost Souls*. It sounded ominous, which might have been intentional but for the cheery twinkle lights outlining it. Emma didn't want to invite too many people to drop in unless they needed help. At least she'd renovated the mansion to get things up and running.

For decades, this place sat empty on the outskirts of town. Old Walter had created an elaborate treasure hunt to find his heir. Participating had become a town tradition, so Rusty and I teamed up. Then we met Emma. When she won the hunt, she not only inherited the house and all the attached cash: she gained witchy powers she'd lost at a young age. Since then, she'd been using the house as a sort of bed and breakfast for people in need.

The first time I'd been here, I'd expected the place to look like the Haunted Mansion at Disneyland. Maybe because I knew a witch lived here. But no. Every time I'd been here over the past few months, the beauty of the house took my breath away.

Part of that was because it looked different each time. Someone had been busy remodeling. Again. The house was bright and airy, largely thanks to the light-colored brick on the outside. Two massive turrets in the front flanked a stone staircase leading up to the double doors with stained glass windows that must be twenty-five feet high. Today, the glass depicted a mermaid swimming through a colorful ocean. The house reportedly had forty-one rooms. The first time Rusty and I had visited, we'd started counting but we quickly lost track. Not that the exact size mattered. The estate was large and gorgeous.

Blue and pink shingles on the roof blended to make a lovely lilac hue visible from down the street. On the left side, a covered porch wrapped around to the back. Knowing how much Emma liked outdoor spaces, I suspected it kept going. We were the only car in the circular driveway, probably because a path off to one side led back to what used to be a barn but was now a modern three-car garage.

As we got out of the car and approached the front, Kevin let out a low whistle. "This place is pretty nice, huh? It looks like Emma's been working hard on renovations."

"I wouldn't say she's been working *hard*, exactly," I said. "Apparently, now that she's got her gifts under control, taking care of the house is a breeze."

My friend Emma had inherited the house from her grandfather, along with the magical gift she'd never known she had. Well, she sort of knew it—Emma thought she had ridiculously bad luck with every spell going wrong, so she didn't do a lot of magic. Then she discovered someone had cursed her and corrupted her powers. But that was all in the past. Now, most of her spells did what she wanted.

"Must be nice," Kevin muttered under his breath. "Does she do laundry?"

"Look, I *promise* I'll take everything out of the dryer when we get home. I thought—"

The front door swung open, and a strawberry-blonde popped into view. "Aly! You don't call, you don't write. Also, you look a fright."

"Does she always speak in rhyme?" Kevin whispered.

"No. I think that was a coincidence," I whispered back. Louder, I said, "This is a bed and breakfast! Aren't your doors always open?"

She shrugged. "That plan is a work in progress. Heavy emphasis on the work. But please, come in. What's going on?"

Emma led us through the foyer while I explained briefly what was happening. When we got to the living room, she stopped and turned, hands on her hips. Her hazel eyes flashed. "Tell me you didn't bring me a cursed bunny who's gonna steal my powers. I lived long enough without them, and I'd rather not go back."

Kevin shook his head. "No, no. We left him in Shady Grove. We just want to see how big this problem is. I need you to lie to me."

"I love it when people drop by my place unannounced," she replied dryly.

"Either that's true, or still nothing," Kevin said. "I have a sneaking suspicion it's the latter."

I sighed and dropped onto the velvet settee. Way more antique and fancy than I'd expect in Emma's house, but Walter left her most of the furniture, too. "This is never going to work."

"I was joking," Emma assured us. "I don't mind you guys being here. I'm surprised, but happy to see you."

"Now you've made two contradictory statements, and neither triggered as a lie," Kevin said. "Is your magic working?"

"Better than ever!" She chirped. "Watch this!"

Emma snapped her fingers. Nothing happened. A look of concern crossed her face. "Oh, no!"

"Not funny." I gave her a withering look. "Just do a spell."

"Any spell at all will do," Kevin added.

"Sorry, I couldn't resist." Her eyes twinkled with merriment. She snapped her fingers, and a small metal tray appeared in her hands. "See that?"

"Are those chocolate chip?" I asked. The tantalizing aroma hit my nose, and it was all I could do not to reach for one before she offered.

"You made us cookies?" Kevin asked.

"Don't be silly. I'd hate to poison you," she said. "I conjured these from the kitchen. I've got this amazing cook now. She's a whiz with baked goods."

"You've hired a cook but you're not running a B&B?"

"It's a long story," she said. "Let's focus. Why are you so concerned about *my* magic? You think whatever's affecting you is contagious?"

Oh, fluorine. That hadn't actually occurred to me. If so, coming here had been a huge mistake.

Kevin stepped forward. "We don't think so, but it's important to cover all the bases."

"And whatever caused this took both your powers at the same time? Could it be like a family power cold?"

"No," I said glumly. "It's affecting Olive, too."

Kevin cleared his throat, and I didn't mention Kyle. Not that I'd been planning to. Emma may be a friend, but I didn't know her that well.

"Oh, wow. What happened?" she said.

"We don't know," Kevin said. "It's been at least forty-eight hours."

"Before now, when was the last time you did magic?" I asked. Maybe it came and went?

She thought for a minute. "Nicole—that's one of the teens staying with me—left for a job interview around three. Before she left, I did a spell to keep her clothes wrinkle free and give her a boost of confidence."

"From having unwrinkled clothes?" I asked.

"No. From the magic. That's two spells."

Kevin said, "You're sure that was this afternoon?"

"Yeah, why?"

"Did you do magic yesterday?"

"Uh-huh. I'm a hearth witch, running a group home. Now that my spells don't all go wrong, I do magic every day."

That made perfect sense. "Sorry. We're trying to pinpoint when we lost our powers. I think it happened around the time I found the bunny. So far, everyone we know was affected has been in direct contact with him."

Quickly, I took her through the scene we'd found at the pet store yesterday morning, the owner's disappearance, and how I became the proud auntie to a gray and white mottled fur bunny. He was growing on me. Too bad I'd have to give him back. And also, if the rabbit's appearance coincided with the loss of our powers, he might be evil.

When I finished, she shook her head. "Only you, Aly. An evil magic bunny?"

"I didn't know Kelvy was evil!"

"Hold up. You named a rabbit *Kelvy*? Were you mad at him?"

I snorted. "It's a long story."

"You knew you were bringing a rabbit into my house," Kevin interjected.

"Hush. Kyle loves him. He's a good pet, unless he's evil."

"Are you sure it's the bunny?" Emma said. "Could there be something else that explains all of this? Some kind of magical event?"

"The earthquake." I glanced at Kevin. "Could the earthquake have caused us to lose our powers?"

Emma blinked at me. "What earthquake?"

"The one in Shady Grove yesterday morning."

"Must have been when I was in my car," she said. "I didn't feel a thing. Weird that no one mentioned it, though. Seems like big news."

Kevin said, "I've never heard of an earthquake causing someone to lose magical powers."

"Where would you read about it, *The New York Times*?" Emma snorted. "Is anyone else affected?"

I ticked off the people we knew about on my fingers. "Us, Olive. I texted Amira but haven't heard back yet."

Kevin looked uneasily between me and Emma. "Maybe we should go. What if this thing is contagious?"

"I'm not sure how it could be," she said. "It's more likely the three of you were in the wrong place at the wrong time. But listen, I'm not sure the answer here is a spell-casting evil rabbit."

"What makes you say that?" Kevin asked.

"That type of spell requires a lot of power," she said. "The fact that it extends miles away from the bunny *and affects multiple people who've had contact with him*? Sounds more like a magical virus. Is there someone you can take him to, get him checked out? It's possible there's a more rational explanation."

"Our magic having a cold is the rational explanation?" Kevin asked. "Life used to be so much easier."

I stuck my tongue out at him. "You're the one who wanted to move to Shady Grove."

"Sorry my wife got murdered," he shot back.

To Emma, I said, "We have a local vet, but I'm not sure she can check a bunny for magic."

A large black cat bounded into the room, interrupting us when he jumped onto Emma's lap. She stroked his head as he gazed into her eyes and started meowing forcefully.

"What is wrong with that cat?" Kevin asked.

"Shh," I said. "Pink is magic."

"You couldn't have mentioned earlier that you had experience with magical animals?" he said.

I shrugged. "It slipped my mind. Good thing we're here, huh?"

While we were bickering, Emma and Pink finished their conversation. He settled down in her lap and started licking one paw.

"Any insight?" I asked her.

"Pink thinks that whatever's going on, it's temporary."

"Hold on," Kevin said. "You can talk to the cat?"

"Sure I can," Emma said. "It's part of my magic. Or his. I'm not clear on that."

"At least we've established that magical animals are a thing," Kevin said.

"I knew that," I said.

"Next time, please consider sharing with the rest of the class."

"The good news," Emma said loudly, "is Pink says if it's a magical cold, maybe there's a cure. But if the bunny *is* doing a spell, he won't be able to maintain it forever. It's too much of a power drain."

"What if the bunny is some kind of damper? Maybe it's not magic so much as... anti-magic?" I wrinkled my nose. That didn't exactly sound like the right word, but they knew what I meant.

Pink meowed again. Emma cocked her head to listen before translating. "It's possible. It's not common, but it could happen."

"How would we know?" Kevin asked.

"How else?" I said with a grin. "The scientific method."

"Only you would get so excited about doing a bunch of experiments without getting college credit," Emma said.

I grinned unabashedly. "I can't wait to get started. Did Pink say what we do if the rabbit is causing our magic loss unintentionally?"

"The first thing to do is remove the rabbit from your house ASAP," Emma said. "Like, yesterday."

"He's currently staying with Julie, but Kevin spends a lot of time at her place. We could take him to the local animal shelter?" I asked. "I think that's in Willow Falls."

"More likely Saratoga," Kevin said.

"Or not so local," Emma said. "If the bunny is doing this and he can't control his magic—or you can't control him—you don't want him anywhere near you."

"Where should he go?" I asked. "Is there a town where no one has magic?"

"Cleveland," she deadpanned. "Seriously, I'll do some research. If your theory is right, Kelvy could hypothetically go stay with a non-magical family. He can live a long and happy bunny life and no one ever needs to know about any of this aside from us."

"And if not?"

She swallowed. "You might need to get used to living a normal life again. Without your powers."

CHAPTER SIXTEEN

KEVIN and I were halfway back to his office when Rusty texted, reminding me that we had an appointment after lunch. He kindly suggested that he would be perfectly happy to cancel, and I was tempted to agree. Now that I knew I wasn't the only Shady Grove resident who lost their powers, it seemed more important than ever to find out what happened.

But Jeff was still missing, and now that I knew the police weren't looking for him, I had to do what I could. Being responsible for his pet rabbit made me more determined to find Jeff alive. Which meant talking to the one person who we knew might benefit if he went missing.

The Nailed It! mobile salon looked only slightly less terrifying than it sounded. It was a large white van without windows and enormous hands painted on the side. It reminded me of that time Kevin made me watch some old sitcom where the main character loved a movie called *Manos: Hands of Fate*. If Rusty and I got massaged to death, Kevin would never let me live it down.

Unlike most nail salons, this one traveled to meet the customers. Since I didn't want Kevin to ask any questions, I had asked Rainbow to meet us outside Rusty's place. The fact that it gave me a chance to knock once again on Jeff's door was only a bonus.

He didn't answer. I sat on the bell, holding it while I slowly recited every single element of the periodic table aloud. No one could ignore that, and if he'd been in the shower, he had plenty of time to get out. He couldn't be in there.

Darn it. Life would be so easy if missing people just showed up when you wanted them to and saved you from having to get a pedicure in a murder van. Or as Kyle would call it, a "murda van."

There wasn't time to explore Jeff's house again, and I didn't see the point. Instead, I went to pick up Rusty for our appointments. He met me at the front door, looking much more fabulous than the last time I saw him.

"Hey, how did things go with the not-cheating wife?"

He kissed my cheek. "I encouraged my client to talk to Tory about her brother. She told him that Jeff had been asking for money, and everyone is happy."

An uneasy feeling came over that. "When was that? Could Tory's husband have caused Jeff's disappearance?"

"I doubt it," Rusty said. "He told me he offered to pay everything, but his wife insisted Jeff needs to learn his lesson. Thaddeus is definitely of the 'you can't take it with you' mindset. He's extremely generous—that's why his kids were worried in the first place. Thad gave me a huge bonus, by the way, so thank you for your help."

"Glad to be of service," I said as we walked toward the sidewalk.

A few steps from the van, Rusty stopped and put one hand on my arm. "Did I ever tell you that I'm going to die before I'm thirty?"

I shot him a curious look. "No...?"

"That's because I fully intend to live to a ripe old age. Which means, I love you, but I am not getting in that death trap."

"What? Come on, don't you want a pedicure on me?"

Rusty glanced down at his feet before meeting my gaze again. "Are you asking if I want to soak my feet in a bucket before someone in a murder van cuts them off?"

I resisted the urge to stomp my feet. "Rusty! You promised you'd come with me."

"Sorry, sweetheart. I think this is your boyfriend's job. Where is Studmuffin Sam, anyway?"

"Working," I said. "He'll be here next week."

"Smart man," Rusty muttered.

"I heard that," I said. "Listen, you might as well come in with me because you'll get all sweaty and gross standing here."

The back door of the van flew open, revealing two big brown leather massage chairs. They had the fluffy armrests and headrests you'd see on those chairs in the mall, but each ended in a large metal tub. Along the far wall, bright lights pointed at a table full of implements that would be terrifying in any van other than one doubling as a nail salon.

Rainbow stood in the doorway, eyes twinkling. "Aly! It's good to see you again. Come in, come in!"

Rusty crossed his arms and eyed her. "Did you kill Jeff?"

I choked on a laugh. "Rusty! You can't just ask her that."

Rainbow snorted. "What are you talking about?"

Rusty glared at me for a long moment. Finally, I shrugged. "Go ahead. It's too late to be coy now."

"Jeff Ahn," he said. "The pet store owner. He's missing, presumed dead."

"Presumed by who?" Rainbow asked.

"Me, obvs," Rusty said. "No one has seen him in more than a day. Anyway, we just want to know if you did it and if you plan to kill us when we climb into your van."

My mouth hung open until he leaned over and gently tapped my chin to shut it.

"What are you doing?" I hissed at him. "Did they teach you this in private investigator school?"

"They taught me to stay alive. That van is a death trap."

"You kids are a hoot," Rainbow said. "Listen, Aly booked two pedicures. If I promise to leave the back door open, will you come on in? I'll tell you what I know about your friend Jeff Ahn."

"We're not friends," Rusty said. "I've never met him. Aly has his pet bunny, and she'd like to return it."

"Preferably before my nephew gets so attached we have to keep it."

Rainbow hopped down and opened the other van door, giving a full view of the interior. A cosmetology license hung on the inside of the door with "Rainbow Wardlaw" and a picture of her unsmiling face. That comforted me somewhat. At least at one point, she knew what she was doing.

I settled myself into the massage chair closer to the front of the van, letting Rusty stay between me and the exit. My best friend hovered while I pressed the buttons until the rollers came to life. As soon as I closed my eyes and let out a sigh of pure joy, Rusty dove into the seat beside me. Apparently, all of his scary thoughts paled in comparison to the reality of a free chair massage.

"So, Rainbow, how long have you been working out of your van?" he asked.

She snorted. "Nice subject change. I moved to Shady Grove about two months ago. Before that, I lived and worked in Rochester. Had a nice little place there. You can google it."

His phone was out practically before she finished her sentence. I swallowed a laugh. "Trust but verify" might as well be Rusty's motto. After a moment, he nodded. "Story checks out. What happened?"

"Oh, same old story." She picked up a jug from a hot plate in the corner and poured warm water over my feet into the tub. It felt heavenly. Then she started rubbing my legs, and in that moment, I'd have told her everything. I made a mental note to look for ways to add massage to my interrogation techniques.

"It was a guy, wasn't it?"

"Actually, the health department shut me down." Rusty shot to his feet, and she let out a huge, braying laugh. "I'm joking. You're too easy, kid."

Rusty muttered under his breath as he eased back into his seat. It was probably better that the mechanical whirl of the chair's motors kept me from hearing his words. "What brought you to Shady Grove?"

"I grew up here," Rainbow said. "Followed my high school boyfriend to Rochester, settled down, started working. We got married, raised kids together. I eventually opened the salon. About six months ago, I caught him with his secretary, and now, here I am. Doing what I love any way I can."

"Can't you open a salon somewhere other than Main Street?" Rusty asked.

"Not in Shady Grove," she sighed. "Not any time soon, at least. The Mayor's Office essentially confirmed they'll never approve me. But I'm working on a plan. Don't worry about me."

"Listen, Rainbow." I leaned forward. "We know you wanted Jeff's storefront. You told me that yourself, and you were upset about the landlord going with someone else. You swore you'd get your revenge. Now Jeff is missing. You have to admit it looks bad."

"What do you care?"

An excellent question. I couldn't exactly explain I'd been helping investigate crimes since realizing I was psychic—especially when my powers had up and ditched me at a very inconvenient time—so I went with a partial truth. "Like Rusty said, I'm caring for his bunny until we find him. I live with my brother, and he's not happy about it."

She snorted, waving the hand that held some kind of stabbing implement. I forced myself not to flinch. "Oh, that. I got my revenge."

I couldn't quite believe we were getting a confession so easily. But I'd already made that mistake with Mellie.

"You're saying you kidnapped Jeff?"

"Don't be dumb. I wasn't mad at him, although he was an easy target. Sorry about losing it in your store."

"That's okay. You didn't blame him for getting the space?"

"Nah. He only took advantage of a good business deal. I was mad at that shady mayor of yours and her unfair business practices. She's the reason I didn't get the place, not him."

"Didn't the owner have any say?" Rusty asked.

"The owner gave me a lease!" Her eyes flashed. "I rented all the equipment—which, by the way, is why you have these lovely chairs. They couldn't be returned. Anyway, I got the loans, got the equipment, set up the bank accounts, and then the paperwork for my business license fell through. First they told me that my name wasn't right for Main Street. Fine. I changed the name. They still didn't like it."

"What was the original name?" Rusty asked.

"Tipsy Turvy Nails. Said it made me sound like a drunk. So I went with Nailed It!." She let out a laugh that turned into more of a cackle. "I love that show. It was so perfect. But no, they said it wasn't the 'right kind of catchy'. Whatever that means. While I was trying to figure out the appeals process, the owner canceled my lease and signed with Jeff. Said he couldn't wait."

"Can they do that?" I asked.

"If I don't have a business to move in? Sure, I guess," Rainbow said. "Anyway, that's when Jeff submitted his application. He got approved immediately. As if Paws and Effect is a better name for a shop than Nailed It!."

"She's got a point," Rusty said to me. "So you were mad. You wanted revenge. What happened?"

"I peed in the fountain in front of City Hall." She picked up a tool and started scraping the bottoms of my feet while Rusty howled with laughter. "Don't tell anyone, it's a three hundred dollar fine."

"Your secret is safe with us," I assured her. "Sorry you didn't get the space. We were hoping to come in."

"Thank you. Jeff didn't do anything but show up in the right place at the right time. At that point, the owner would've given my space to anyone City Hall approved. All because the mayor's overcharging, pretentious sister can't handle a little fair competition."

She rattled on, talking about how the nail salon in Willow Falls was far inferior to hers while she worked on my feet, then Rusty's. We let her talk. Most of what she said fit with what I knew about Mayor Banister. It made sense.

"Anyway, if you want to know what I think, I bet it was that sleazy guy. TJ something."

That caught my attention.

"The reporter?" Rusty asked.

"Yeah. He was lurking around the store. Around the time I was at Missing Pieces. Listen, nothing interesting ever happens in Shady Grove." Rusty and I exchanged a look but didn't comment. Bent over my feet, Rainbow didn't notice. She continued, "I think he staged a robbery at the pet store so he'd have something to write about. Jeff caught him, and TJ had to get him out of the way."

There were worse reasons to kill someone.

"Out of the way?" Rusty asked, picking up the same phrasing I did. "You think Jeff is dead?"

"Well, if he's not, where is he? There are only so many places you can stash a grown man around here. No one happened to see anyone dragging an unconscious guy up and down Main Street, did they?"

"Uh, no. Not to my knowledge," I said. "Amira and I were both headed to the pet store right before the earthquake, and neither of us saw anyone."

"You raise a good point," Rusty said, "But if Jeff was dead, whoever killed him would still have to take him out of the store, right?"

"Bodies can be moved in pieces," Rainbow said decisively. I

was about to take Rusty's belated advice and get the heck out of the van when she added, "I saw it on *Dexter*."

Something occurred to me. "Do you know if the pet store has a basement?"

Rusty spoke up. "None of the businesses on Main Street have basements. After the Great Maple Syrup Incident of 1814, the ground was too hard to dig. The stores have basic concrete slabs and that's it. Didn't you ever notice Missing Pieces didn't have one?"

I shook my head. "We have a storage room. No one has basements in my part of California; I didn't think about it. So much for that theory."

"Don't worry, sweetie. You'll think of something," Rainbow said, patting my shin. She went on and on, sharing one theory after another that implicated everyone from the Chief of Police in Willow Falls to Dr. Younger the veterinarian to Patti at the diner. ("Come on, you can't tell me that's ground beef in her meatloaf.")

Rusty and I pretended to hang on every word, but it didn't take long to realize that she was just tossing out baseless accusations. Rainbow might be a pretty decent cosmetologist, but she'd never be a detective.

This non-magical private investigator stuff was for the birds. For the first time, I wondered why Rusty even wanted to get a license. We could have saved so much time if I could've just had a vision show me where Jeff went.

Forty minutes later, Rusty and I left the salon sporting matching fabulous blue toenails and defeated expressions. We were pretty sure Rainbow wasn't responsible for Jeff's disappearance, but that really put a damper on our suspect list.

At this rate, we'd never figure out what happened to Jeff. Or my powers.

CHAPTER SEVENTEEN

MY DAMPENED SPIRITS thankfully only lasted a few minutes. Say what you would about Shady Grove, but we had the best grapevine. Town gossip Thelma Reyes made it her business to know everything about everyone, and she always delivered her news with a dramatic flair. No surprise, really. She'd made a name for herself acting on a soap opera for about forty years before she retired and moved here. If anyone would know whether Rainbow's claims about the permits were true, it was Thelma.

Months ago, I'd accidentally discovered that the only thing Thelma loved more than gossip was baked goods. Before dropping by her house, I stopped at Let's Bake a Deal to pick up four cupcakes with a kick—Tony's late summer specialty came with a mint-julep theme in honor of the track. Vanilla cakes, complete with bourbon and crème de menthe. Nothing like boozy baked goods to make someone happy.

Shady Grove's pre-eminent gossip lived in a fabulously pink house. Her perfectly manicured lawn put the lawn maintenance crew at the nearby golf course to shame.

Thelma opened her front door with a smile, wearing a flowered yellow housecoat and enough makeup for a red carpet event. She never let anyone see her without putting her face on. Her newly pink-tinged hair hung in tight pin curls below her chin. When she saw the white bakery box in my hands, her smile widened.

"Come in, come in!"

I followed Thelma to her living room while she went to get tea and plates. One of the first things she ever said to me was to always keep a kettle on, just in case, and I'd never been disappointed. Thelma loved serving tea almost as much as she loved sharing the latest tidbits.

A moment later, she returned bearing a silver tea tray, two beautiful pink china cups, a matching teapot, and the cupcakes on two plates. If I were the type of person who took pictures of their food, I'd be uploading that scene in a heartbeat. Thelma perched on the edge of the couch, handed me a cup and saucer, and waited for me to look at her before speaking. She was used to commanding people's attention.

"Good morning, Aluminum." I'd long since given up trying to get her to use my nickname, so I didn't correct her. "Lovely picture of you in the *Sentinel* this morning."

"Ugh. I only met TJ yesterday morning, but apparently he has it out for me."

With a smug smile, Thelma sipped her tea. "TJ Crews grew up in Shady Grove. When his parents divorced he moved to Indiana with his mother, but he came back in high school. Recently graduated Maloney College and came to work at the newspaper."

"Maloney? Do we even have a journalism department?"

"I don't think so, dear," she said. "TJ's dad runs the paper. He couldn't find a job in the area after college, probably because he failed most of his classes."

Working as a local reporter seemed like a good job, but I could see him being bitter if he'd wanted a science-based career. Not that his issues made it okay to tell the whole town that chaos followed me. It wasn't like I blew up the pet store. Being outside a building when an earthquake hit wasn't suspicious, it was bad luck.

"Anyway, TJ isn't interesting," she said. "He didn't have anything to write about in this small town, so he picked you."

"He could have written about the missing pet store owner," I grumbled.

"True enough," she said. Then she leaned forward conspiratorially, as if we weren't the only two people in the house. "Do you know what happened to Jeff?"

"Not a clue. I don't suppose you've talked to him? You were my best hope."

She preened at my words for a few seconds before her smile drooped. "I'm afraid not, dear. The only time I spoke with Jeff was Friday. He was standing by the loading dock at Paws and Effect to oversee the delivery of his inventory. The animals hadn't arrived yet, but he said he was concerned about possible vandalism."

"From Rainbow, I bet." I clapped one hand over my mouth. "Sorry, I shouldn't have said that."

As expected, my fake faux pas was exactly what Thelma needed to tell me more.

She said, "You're not telling me anything he didn't say personally. Seemed a little paranoid to be honest, but I don't judge. It's just terrible what happened. An earthquake in Shady Grove! Whoever heard of such a thing?"

That got me thinking. "How long have you lived here?"

"Only a few years, since I retired. I used to act on *As the Hospital Guides Our Lives*, you know." She said this as if anyone could ever forget.

"A few years? I thought Julie said you and her aunt go way back." The local coffee shop used to be called A Hill of Beans. When Julie's aunt passed away, she inherited it. Left her law practice in New York and moved north.

"Oh, well, sure," Thelma said. "My grandmother lived here when I was a kid. In this very house. My family used to visit every summer. Never experienced an earthquake, though. I didn't even feel this one. Perhaps I'm just too well grounded. What do you think happened?"

"Global warming?" She snorted, so I decided to change the subject rather than explain the science. "Do you know where Jeff was before the earthquake hit? I was on my way to the store when the tremors started, but he wasn't inside when I got there."

She shook her head. "No one has said anything to me. To be honest, hardly anyone is talking about the earthquake. I heard about it from Amira Patel at the magic store. Lovely girl."

I resisted the urge to point out that Amira was at least twenty-five. Not exactly a girl. Sometimes talking to Thelma felt like riding a bike in a hurricane. "Do you know anyone who would want to hurt Jeff? Is it true that Rainbow Wardlaw was supposed to get the space and he stole it out from under her?"

Thelma waved one hand. "That woman is never going to settle anywhere. She flits in and out of town, moving where the spirit takes her. She might have applied for a business license, but she never would have stayed for long."

"Are you sure? She seemed pretty upset to miss out."

"Oh, she was mad, sure enough. Ellie told me someone egged the mayor's house when Jeff got the lease."

"Ellie?"

She pointed vaguely to the east and I remembered Thelma's new neighbor. Her daughter worked as an aide for Mayor Banister, so she would know. I made a mental note to drop by and talk to her.

"You think Rainbow egged the mayor's house?" I didn't see why she was any more likely than any other resident of the town. Mostly because vandalizing Mayor Banister's home *and* desecrating the town's fountain seemed like overkill. But I'd promised to keep Rainbow's secret, so I didn't say anything more.

"If you ask me, the person you should be talking to is TJ." I tried not to show my disgust but clearly, it shone through in my expression. "Sorry. He covers City Hall. He's the one in the know."

Mentally I added talking to TJ to my "when hell freezes over" list. But her words reminded me of something: City Hall issued all the permits, which were available to the public. I could check the records. Maybe someone other than Jeff and Rainbow had applied. That space was prime Shady Grove real estate. It wouldn't surprise me if multiple people wanted it.

I peered toward the house next door. "Do you think Ellie's home? I'd love to meet her."

"My dearest, I could see through you without my reading glasses. You want to pump Ellie for information, be my guest." Thelma picked up the phone and made a quick call before going into the kitchen to get another cupcake and tea cup. A moment later, she returned with both, plus a tall, thin black woman with short gray hair who she introduced as Ellie.

"It's nice to meet you," I said. "How do you like your new home?"

"Oh, it's wonderful. Plenty of room for my grandsons to run around, and it was empty for so long, I got it for a *steal*."

Part of me wondered if the low price had more to do with living beside the town gossip rather than how long it took to find a buyer. As the former owner's brother and closest relative, Rusty's father had inherited the property. He offered to let his only son move in. Rusty said there wasn't enough money in the world to live with Thelma's nose pressed up against his windows all day and night.

"You're not worried about what happened to the former owner?" I asked, only half-joking. While I'd never met a ghost, I'd learned to remain open to the possibilities. Rumor had it the only bar in Shady Grove had closed down because it was haunted. Or cursed.

She waved one hand. "Don't be ridiculous. Amira did a cleansing for me. I'm fine."

Eventually, I steered the conversation toward Ellie's kids, and specifically her daughter's job working for Mayor Banister. "Does Janie help with issuing business permits? I heard there was some big deal a few weeks ago."

"Technically, it's the City Clerk who has that job," Ellie said. "But my Janie is such a good girl, they keep giving her more and more responsibility. So many people inquired about that space, they put her in charge of the Town Hall Meeting about it last month."

Interesting. Was that normally something the Mayor's personal aide would help with? I suspected not. It didn't make any sense that she would need to discuss the permits with anyone in advance. How did she help Jeff make it go through? I needed to know exactly what happened during that conversation.

Was he able to pay for the permits? Did his sister cover the cost, like she was paying for everything else? Because it didn't make any sense for the landlord to give the place to Jeff over Rainbow if he couldn't even afford the business license.

Something didn't add up.

CHAPTER EIGHTEEN

AFTER FINISHING my truly amazing cupcake, I went to City Hall. On my only previous visit, I'd overheard Mayor Banister insist Sheriff Matthews arrest Olive despite having little evidence of wrongdoing, so this place didn't exactly fill me with warm, fuzzy feelings.

My first stop was the Clerk's Office on the second floor. A sign on the wall outside the door told me that inside I would find not only the Clerk but the Register of Deeds, the Tax Assessor, the Town Enforcement Officer, and the Comptroller.

I walked inside, expecting to see a room full of desks. Instead, a counter separated one man with dark brown hair and bronze skin from the waiting area. He typed so fast I expected smoke to rise from his keyboard. A nameplate on the desk identified him as Manuel Garcia, Comptroller.

"Good morning. How can I help you?"

"I'm Aly Reynolds."

"Ah, yes. The lawyer's sister."

At this point, I'd learned not to be surprised. There were no strangers in Shady Grove, only people who'd heard of you but not yet introduced themselves. Still, this might be a good way to open the lines of communication. "You know Kevin?"

"Sure. He's in my bowling league."

Of course he was. Apparently I was the only person in Shady Grove who didn't bowl. The local alley, We All Fall Down, was the town hotspot before the owner went to jail at the beginning of the year. After it sat empty for a few months, his brother moved to town to take over. Once again, residents filled the place night after night, especially on the weekends.

"I'll have to watch a tournament sometime," I said, knowing it was less likely than combining hydrogen and oxygen to make milk. "Do you know where I can find the Clerk?"

"Yes, I do!" He rolled the nameplate on his desk twice. I hadn't noticed that it was multi-sided. Now it read "Manuel Garcia, Town Clerk."

"Can you tell me how many people applied for a permit to operate a business at 15 Main Street?"

"The new pet store?" When I nodded, he said, "sure thing. Let me pull that up."

He began typing again, fingers blurring. After a minute, he furrowed his brow. "You sure about that address?"

"I am," I said. "15 Main Street. It was empty for a while, but now it's Paws and Effect."

Manuel pressed a button, then hit enter. Again. Then he clicked around several times. Finally, he met my eyes. "The last permit I show for that address was issued in 1982. A tourist shop. Sold all kinds of t-shirts and knickknacks. But it closed about four years ago."

"Nothing more recent?"

He shook his head.

"Can a person rent a commercial property and start a business without a license?"

"No. Town regulations require approval, partially to ensure compliance with the naming convention. The owner would get fined for leasing to anyone who didn't get approved by us."

"Do you remember anyone applying for that space? Or multiple someones?"

"No, but I haven't been here for the past few months. I got called to jury duty down in Albany. Big federal case. Financial fraud. Fascinating stuff, really."

"Who covers for you when you're gone?" I tried to recall all the job titles posted outside. "The Registrar of Deeds?"

He flipped the nameplate again to "Manuel Garcia, Registrar of Deeds."

"No, that's also me. I don't have a second-in-command. We don't get a lot of business here most of the time, so Mayor Banister's aide took over. Janie Something. She's lovely. If you ask me, her talents are wasted in the mayor's office."

All roads pointed back to Janie. Huh.

Trying not to let my frustration show, I thanked him and asked for directions to Janie's office. He pointed me down the stairs, to the office just past the restroom. I should've known that was the mayor's office. It made sense that her aide would work near her.

Bypassing the elevator, I headed toward the stairwell. Once inside, I leaned back against the wall and closed my eyes, reviewing everything I knew.

Jeff was missing, Rainbow wanted his space, and TJ was obnoxious. The permit applications for Paws and Effect had vanished, assuming they existed in the first place, and the federal courts did jury duty. A whole lot of nothing.

Element one was hydrogen. Element two was helium. Helium made your voice high and squeaky, kind of like Rainbow's. That wasn't helpful.

I could do this. Wiping my sweaty palms on my pants, I swung the door open and went in. The mayor's office didn't look all that different on the inside from Manuel's, except for the closed door on the right-hand wall with a frosted glass window on the top and the words "Mayor's Office" etched into it.

At a desk behind the counter, I spotted a black woman wearing wire-rimmed glasses, her dark red hair pulled back in a low bun at the nape of her neck. She wore a blue shirt buttoned to her chin and typed away steadily, gazing at her computer screen with the single-minded determination of a marathon runner.

According to Rainbow, Janie had accepted a bribe to give the business permit to Jeff instead of her. Ellie's comments didn't exactly contradict that. But Janie certainly didn't look like someone who broke the rules. I didn't think they needed the money, either. Although Thelma had told me a few months ago that Janie and her husband had four kids, he worked as the manager at the Shady Grove Credit Union.

She looked up when I approached. "Can I help you?"

"I hope so." I took a deep breath. "My name is Aly Reynolds, and I work at Missing Pieces on Main Street. Not far from the new pet store."

"The pet store debate is closed," she said. "Any concerns should be taken up directly with the owner or brought to the attention of the City Council at the next open meeting in November."

Big help, since that was ten weeks away.

"My concern is that Jeff is missing," I said.

"The sheriff's office is next door," she said, still not meeting my gaze. "Go now, before he heads out to lunch."

Janie's mom was so lovely, I'd expected her daughter to be a bit warmer. Or at least marginally polite.

Ignoring her suggestion, I took a deep breath. Go big or go home, right? "Some people are saying Jeff paid you to give him the business license instead of Rainbow."

Finally, the typing stopped. Janie swiveled around in her chair. "I don't know who you've been talking to—"

"Your mother said you'd met with Jeff before the final decision was made. She was so proud of you."

"I see." Janie smiled thinly. "Mayor Banister asked me to meet with both candidates for that space before we issued a permit."

She didn't seem to be hiding anything. Not even the fact that she had better things to do than explain herself to me. "Were there only two applications?"

"Only two people filed, yes."

Now we were getting somewhere. "Can you tell me what helped you make your final decision?"

"Certainly. Mr. Ahn was the only one to submit a complete application." At my surprised look, she gave a hollow laugh. "I know you fancy yourself some kind of super sleuth, Ms. Reynolds, but not everything has a sinister motive. Ms. Wardlaw submitted her paperwork without the required supporting documentation and fee. Mr. Ahn did not."

"How much is the fee?" I asked. If Jeff had been saving up to pay the fees for a while, that could explain why he was behind on his other bills.

"If you want to apply for a business permit, I'll have to direct you to the second floor," Janie replied. "I'm sorry, but we're very busy here. Mayor Banister has a full schedule. It's time for you to go stir up trouble somewhere else."

Oh, fluorine. Now I knew what this was about. "You didn't happen to read this morning's *Shady Grove Sentinel*, did you? Because what TJ wrote—"

"Is there anything else I can help you with?"

"Do you know what happens to the permit applications after they're submitted?" I asked.

She spoke as if addressing a very small child. "Each application is either approved or denied. Now, if you're done wasting my time—"

"No, you misunderstood me," I said. "Once the decision is made, where do the applications go? How long does it take to get the permits issued? I was just upstairs and they didn't have any record at all of any recent permits or requests."

Janie's eyes widened. "That's not funny."

"I'm serious." I gestured to her phone. "Call Manuel Garcia."

She was already lifting the phone to her ear. "Manuel, hi! Janie here. Hold on a second." Then she paused, covering the receiver with one hand. "Did you need anything else?"

That was a fine thank you. I gave her an important tip, and she shooed me out like a housefly. But unloading my righteous indignation was only going to get me a security escort. Besides, if she found the permits, then I could read them.

With nothing else to do and Janie glaring at me steadily, I thanked her and left.

On my way out, I passed Mayor Banister, who paid zero attention to me. Wondering if I would overhear anything of interest, I flattened myself against the wall outside and waited. It had worked once, so maybe lightning would strike twice. I needed to find out the application fees, but there was no hurry.

Actually, the clerk probably listed their business license application fees on their website. I really should look it up right away. While standing outside the office door where someone might say something incriminating.

Mayor Banister approached from the other side and threw the door open, acting as if she hadn't noticed me. Janie abruptly hung up her phone to greet her boss. The two of them exchanged pleasantries about the morning schedule. This was probably not my best idea. At least my googling revealed that the application fee cost a whopping twenty-five dollars. Another dead end.

Why was Jeff so broke? Was it just from buying all the inventory and fixing up the space?

Suddenly, music blasted out of my pocket, reverberating off the walls before bouncing back to me. The hallway felt like being at a dance club.

Oh, fluorine.

I'd forgotten to put my phone on silent. Kevin's familiar ringtone usually made me smile, but as the voices inside the office cut off abruptly, I felt nothing but mild irritation. So much for gathering useful information.

Beside me, the wooden door closed firmly yet quietly, leaving me alone with my still-ringing phone. Although I preferred to send it to voicemail, Kyle might need me.

Trying not to sound annoyed, I answered. "What's up, dear Brother?"

"What's your plan for the bunny?"

"Well, I was going to take him to dinner and a show, but that doesn't start until seven."

"Ha ha," he said without a trace of humor. "Seriously, you can't keep this rabbit."

"Yeah, I know. I thought he'd be okay at Julie's for the rest of the day. I'm still trying to find Jeff." Kevin wouldn't appreciate me skulking around City Hall and eavesdropping, so I didn't mention the details.

"He's not great. Julie said the poor little guy has been shrieking all morning. Nothing seems to calm him except showing videos of you on her phone."

"Seriously? That's the strangest thing I've ever heard."

"You're psychic," he replied dryly. "Surrounded by magical people."

"Touché." I thought for a minute. "So you called because Kelvy misses me?"

"No, I called because he started kicking little rabbit turds out of his cage onto Julie's hardwood floors, and while she loves me and really likes you, I don't want her to be tortured by that rabbit for another night."

Ew.

"Sorry about that."

"Don't be sorry. Come get him."

"But what if he's the reason we've lost our powers?"

"Then, according to Emma's cat, he'll run out of power soon and we'll be back to normal." Kevin paused. "I can't believe I just said that. Listen, I know it's a risk, but Julie's afraid the little guy is going to hurt himself."

I felt a twinge of guilt. "Fine. Sorry. I'll see you in twenty minutes."

Resistance was futile. Kevin gave me a place to live rent-free while I went to school. He co-signed for my car. He was family, and over the past two years, he'd also grown into one of my closest friends. If the rabbit bothered his girlfriend, the little guy couldn't stay with her.

"I'm on my way. I'll figure something out," I said.

I hung up the phone before he could ask what time I'd be home. I had other stops to make first. With another long, futile glance at Mayor Banister's office, I pulled my hair up off my neck, adjusted my sunglasses, and headed out.

CHAPTER NINETEEN

BEFORE SWINGING by the coffee shop to get Kelvy, I went back to Paws and Effect. Thelma saw Jeff at the loading dock the day before he went missing. Maybe one of the neighboring store owners witnessed something?

Luckily, City Hall to Main Street wasn't far. Practically before I finished marveling at how short the walk was, Paws and Effect came into view.

To the left was a clothing store I'd never paid much attention to because they specialized in maternity wear. It was called Mamma Mia!, and if they played any music other than songs from the musical, I would be disappointed.

Before going inside, I went around the back. The alley looked pretty much like an empty street on a cool August morning. Bleak. Lifeless. A dumpster sat beside the back door to Paws and Effect, and I debated briefly whether I wanted to look inside.

On the one hand, there could be evidence. On the other, I might find a dead body.

No, wait. Police tape lay on the ground. The wind must have blown it loose, but they'd definitely roped this section off and labeled it a crime scene.

Instead of convincing me to leave the dumpster alone, that gave me the courage to search it. After all, the sheriff would have noticed if Jeff were inside. But I might find something mundane they had overlooked.

Wrinkling my nose, I moved toward the giant blue bin. The black lid was shut, but not locked. After glancing up and down to make sure no one else was around, I swung the right side open. And immediately realized my mistake. Without a ladder, the only way to see anything in there was to hop over the top and dive in. Which one hundred percent was not happening. Not when the dumpster served a place containing approximately twenty-five cat boxes and at least a dozen hamsters. Luckily, a couple of empty milk crates stood behind the adjacent store. I dragged them over and climbed up. Much better.

The dumpster, not surprisingly, smelled like feces and dog food. Also, it was empty. Either Jeff hadn't gotten a chance to use it since moving into the space, or I'd missed the pickup. Slowly, I lowered myself to the ground before closing the lid.

It dropped onto the metal top with a thunk that could be heard in Schenectady. My heart pounded. I counted the first thirty elements before it slowed enough that I felt confident no one had heard me. Time to go.

I dragged the milk crates back where I found them, just in case. As I stood up, my elbow hit the lid of one of the store's metal trash cans, sending it clanging to the ground.

Ow.

This covert stuff was for the birds. I picked up the lid, elbow still smarting. Then I spotted a piece of pink carbon paper lying on top of the stack. *Application for Business Permit.*

Another one? Quickly, I scanned the document. Apparently, the owner of Mamma Mia!—Whitney Hunter—had requested a permit for the empty store, looking to expand their business. According to the bottom of the document, pink was the copy for the applicant, with white to be filed. The white page was still attached. For whatever reason, Whitney must've decided not to move forward.

As I was debating whether to return the permit to the trash or take it with me, the back door to Paws and Effect flew open.

My head shot up at the sound. Jeff was back!

No. No, he wasn't.

A woman who looked around Kevin's age stood in the doorway, with chin-length dark brown hair, large round glasses, and a white lab coat. She had one of those faces where she definitely reminded me of someone, but I was pretty sure we'd never met.

She startled at the sight of me, her olive-skinned face going pale. "May I help you?"

Hiding my bounty behind my back, I shoved the papers into the back of my yoga pants. Hopefully, the trash cans hid my movements. As I racked my brain for any logical reason for being in the alley, I realized that the woman's voice sounded familiar. "Dr. Younger?"

After a moment, she said, "Yes? And you are...?"

"Aly Reynolds," I said. "I'm the one who called you about Jeff's disappearance."

"Oh, right. I'm just finishing up my rounds here. Did you need something?"

I pressed at the ground with the toe of my boot, searching for an excuse that seemed believable. "To be honest, I was hoping Jeff had miraculously reappeared and no one told me. I've been taking care of his bunny, and my brother's not thrilled about it."

"Ah. I saw your note. But no Jeff, I'm afraid. I hope he's okay." Dr. Younger stepped through the door, pulling it firmly shut behind her. "Walk with me. We'll talk about how to help the rabbit and your brother get used to each other."

Although that wasn't why I'd come, I wasn't going to turn down the advice. Together, we walked to Dr. Younger's practice, a few blocks away in a residential neighborhood. By the time we arrived, I knew a lot more about rabbits and new pets. Too bad I didn't want a new pet—I wanted to find the guy who owned him.

When we arrived, I thanked the veterinarian sincerely. She was doing me a huge favor, and we barely knew each other. Then I turned and headed back to Main Street, both happy with what I'd learned and frustrated that once again, I'd failed to find any information that might lead to Jeff.

My phone rang when I was nearing the front door of Mamma Mia!.

"Kevin! It's delightful to hear from you."

"Why aren't you here yet?" he asked. "The rabbit's disturbing customers, so I'm hanging out with him in the apartment while Julie works. I can't leave for my office until this rabbit is gone, and I have an appointment at two-thirty."

The answer to that was because I'd yet to even consider heading in the direction of On What Grounds?. There were too many other things to do first. But my brother wouldn't like hearing that. "Sorry, I got hung up. Dr. Younger was teaching me about bunny care."

"I'll see you in ten minutes," he said.

No, he wouldn't, but instead of arguing, I dropped the phone back in my bag and shut it off. Sorry, Kev. He'd thank me when I found Jeff alive and gave the bunny back.

The inside of Mamma Mia! looked inviting and warm. It had bright lights and row after row of colorful skirts and blouses. Fancier than what I normally wore, but pregnant business-women needed clothes, too.

"Good afternoon, dear." A woman in a slim-fitting, knee-length magenta skirt and a white and magenta-striped blouse approached me. This woman appeared a bit older than Julie, but not as old as Olive. Probably early forties. She was rail-thin and had white hair pulled up on her head in a sleek topknot. A single strand of pearls hung around her neck. This woman's appearance, more than anything, told me that I absolutely couldn't afford the clothes in this place. So much for that cover story.

"Hi," I said, letting her take the lead.

"Are you expecting?"

I laughed. "Oh, no. I'm much too young for that."

Her expression betrayed nothing. "You'd be surprised. How can I help you?"

"Actually, I'm looking for the owner. Whitney?"

She drew herself to her full height. "Who wants to know?"

"I'm Aly Reynolds," I said. "I heard the shop owner was looking to expand into the space next door, and I wondered if she might be hiring."

Please forgive me, Olive.

The woman softened visibly. An expression that might have been a smile tugged at her lips. "I'm sorry, dear, but I'm not expanding at the moment."

"Oh, that's too bad." I hoped to sound concerned and not happy for the opening. "What happened?"

"A woman calling herself Rainbow offered me a thousand dollars not to file the application. She wanted to open a nail salon. We even talked about sharing promotions. Buy a dress, get ten percent off a manicure, things like that."

If Rainbow was paying other people not to seek the space, that gave her another reason to be angry when Jeff got the lease over her. She hadn't mentioned it when we talked, and that once again catapulted her to the top of my suspect list.

"Oh, wow. Why didn't she move in?" I asked.

"City Hall denied the permits. Said we needed to diversify our businesses more." She shuddered. "What were they thinking, putting a *pet store* beside my couture maternity wear? All of my customers are going to run away when they realize my store smells like wet dog."

I took a deep breath, taking in the soothing scent of lavender air freshener. "If it helps at all, I don't smell a thing."

Whitney gave me a withering look. "Pregnancy enhances your olfactory sense."

Right. Okay, then. Mentally, I added Whitney to my list of suspects. She didn't want Jeff to open a pet store, and now he was missing. Her reason for abandoning the application made sense, but that didn't mean it was true. And it didn't mean she wanted Paws and Effect to go in beside her. If she thought the pet store would hurt business, she had a strong motive for keeping it closed. Although you'd think she would attack before the pet store opened, not immediately after.

"Do you know where I could find Jeff?" I asked.

She shook her head. "I haven't seen him since before the earthquake. He dropped in to say hello, he got a phone call, and he rushed out. That was it."

A-ha! A clue. "Do you know who he was talking to?"

She met my eyes squarely. "I'm not a gossip, young lady."

"Of course not, ma'am," I said, reaching for a white lie. "I didn't mean to imply that at all. No one has seen Jeff in two days. I'm just trying to help find him. I've been taking care of his pet rabbit, and the poor thing isn't doing well. He's so sad, I just want to help him find his owner."

"A pet rabbit? What will they think of next?" She rolled her eyes so far back, I wondered if she could see the inside of her skull. Whitney looked around, then dropped her voice. "Listen. You didn't hear it from me, but when he answered the phone, Jeff said, 'Hi, sis.'"

Tory again. Sure, they were related, but when we spoke earlier, she didn't mention that she'd talked to him only a few hours before his disappearance. What else was she hiding?

Mentally kicking myself for dismissing her so easily, I was pulling out my phone to text Rusty for Tory's number when the ticking clock on the wall caught my eye. Uh-oh. I'd been gone much too long.

Kevin was going to be livid. At this rate, I'd be lucky if he didn't tell Julie to put the rabbit on the front stoop and then change our locks.

Hoping that I didn't appear rude, I thanked Whitney and rushed out.

CHAPTER TWENTY

BY THE TIME I picked up Kelvy from Julie's apartment and went to relieve Mrs. Patel from baby-sitting, I was exhausted.

About ten minutes after putting Kyle to sleep, my phone rang. As usual, seeing Sam's picture on the display made my face light up.

I swiped to accept the call. "Using the phone as a phone? To what do I owe this pleasure?"

Sam snorted. "Do you have a few minutes?"

"For you? Always," I said.

"Always? Even when you're out solving mysteries?"

"I plead the fifth."

"I deserve that. But, listen. I found the video."

"You got it!" The words escaped me in a shriek so loud, I clapped one hand over my mouth. No one was around, though. "Did you watch it?"

"Not yet. I figured I could share my screen and we'd watch it together. I'm texting you a link, though, so you can download it later."

"You're amazing. Thank you."

"Don't thank me yet. It could be entirely useless."

"And I'll still appreciate you getting it for me," I said. "Hang on, I'm going to call you from my tablet so I can see better."

"You might want to also grab a drink. It's over an hour."

I lifted my giant iced coffee and tilted it toward the camera. "I'm all set."

Pushing the pile of books on my bed to one side, I arranged the pillows and sat cross-legged. My phone went on the nightstand, and I pulled my tablet into my lap. A series of taps, and Sam's face once again filled my screen.

"How are you watching this?" I asked. "Your laptop doesn't have a DVD player."

"I downloaded it to a flash drive at the school's computer lab. Took about ten minutes."

The school's computer lab was on campus, about fifteen minutes from Sam's apartment, which was already an hour away from the storage place. He didn't have any reason to go there until the fall semester started. My smile let him know that I appreciated how much he was downplaying the time required. He was supposed to be working, and instead he'd spent half the day going to a storage unit and converting files to help me solve a two-year-old murder.

The video opened from the back of the church, with classical piano music quietly playing. Kevin stood at the head of the aisle with a priest and his groomsmen: his two childhood best friends, our dad, and his roommate from his first year in college.

Sam fast-forwarded through a few people trickling in, including my mom and me. After we took our seats, the music changed. Katrina's bridesmaids started to file in to the church. Nothing interesting yet.

"You might as well keep fast-forwarding," I said. "I was at the ceremony, and nothing unusual happened."

"Did anything big almost happen?"

"What do you mean?" I asked.

"You know, like someone tripping and nearly knocking the

cake over. Someone getting plastered but being escorted out before making a scene. The kind of thing Priscilla might have wanted to be there to avoid, if she'd had a vision about it."

I contemplated that for a long moment. "Not that I remember. That seems like something the videographers would edit out, though. At the moment, I'm looking for a woman with the same tattoo as the bridesmaids."

"You want to see if Mallory could be the person from your vision?"

"Exactly."

The ceremony sped by my view. Finally, the priest pronounced Kevin and Katrina spouses for life, and they turned to walk out. I leaned closer to the screen, scanning desperately for a woman with a cast on one leg. She had to be there.

There. Finally. When nearly everyone had filed out, someone in the front row stood and grabbed a pair of crutches that must have been on the bench beside her. A man was with her, helping her move down the row to the aisle. When they got there, the two of them turned. As they grew closer, my pulse quickened.

It was tough to gauge her exact height because the woman was using crutches. She appeared to be a few inches shorter than the man she was with. A quick glance at her feet revealed that she hadn't tried to manipulate crutches in high heels. A wise move on her part.

"That's her," I said. "It has to be."

"Do you think she could be the person who killed Katrina?"

"It's hard to say."

It felt weird to say it, but part of me wanted her to be. I didn't want the killer to be Kyle's aunt or his mother's cousin. We had so little family and either of the Towne women would be able to help him with his powers as he got older.

The tops of the pews were slightly above the woman's hips. She might be taller than Katrina—one of my only two clues from my vision. The killer was taller than Katrina and had the ivy and leaf tattoo that Mary and Priscilla both had on their forearms.

As they grew closer to the camera, I scanned, looking for anything else that might help me determine her height. Toward the end of the aisle, the woman paused to catch her breath. She pushed her chin-length brown hair out of her face, then straightened, shaking her head as if to send her fatigue shimmying to the ground. In doing so, she faced the camera head-on.

I choked.

"What's wrong?" Sam asked.

"I know her," I said. "But her name's not Mallory."

"What are you talking about?"

"That's the local veterinarian. The one who's been taking care of the animals at Paws and Effect for me. Dr. Younger."

CHAPTER TWENTY-ONE

"SAM, I'm sorry, but I have to go." If Mallory was here in town, and she was concealing that fact from me, she had an awful lot of explaining to do.

"Aly. Wait." Sam's tone stopped me in my tracks. "You can't run off without a plan. This woman could be dangerous."

"She was helping me find Mary and Priscilla."

"So she says," he pointed out. "She also lied about who she was. It would have been so easy for her to tell you the truth when you spoke the other night instead of claiming to live in Boston. Or mentioning when you called her to watch the animals that she knew you?"

"Maybe she didn't realize it," I said. "Reynolds is a common name. There's no reason one of Katrina's friends would remember Kevin's little sister."

"A valid point," he conceded. "But what about when you ran into her? You don't look that different."

"I didn't recognize her. It was years ago," I insisted.

"She knew your name by then," Sam pointed out. "And she knew Kevin's sister's name."

He was raising good arguments, but I didn't let them deter me. "She must have had a reason for not wanting me to know."

"What are you going to say? What are you going to do if she tries to snap your neck?"

Closing my eyes, I summoned a mental image of Dr. Younger. From when I saw her in the alley, not the wedding video. She'd been fairly close to my height. The woman who killed Katrina was tall, at least five-foot-ten. Much taller than Mallory.

I opened my eyes and met Sam's gaze in the tablet. He'd shut off the screen-sharing after I dropped my bombshell. "It's not her. She's not tall enough, and her skin is too dark. The woman in my vision was extremely pale, and Dr. Younger's got an olive complexion."

"Okay, then." He swallowed. "I just want you to be safe. It kills me to be so far away, knowing you might be in danger."

"That's why your mom is teaching me self-defense," I said. "I'll be okay. If anything happens, the veterinary clinic is on Third Street."

"Text me in thirty minutes or I'm sending the police over."

Ignoring a twinge of irritation, I promised. No matter how many times I told myself he was just showing how much he cared, I hated when Sam got protective of me. I was my own person, and I could take care of myself.

Luckily, Kevin's bowling league had ended early, so he was home when I finished brushing my hair and preparing for a confrontation. I found him in the kitchen on my way to the garage.

"Where are you headed so late?" he asked.

I hesitated. "If you don't ask me that, I don't have to lie."

"Aly—"

One upraised hand stopped him. "Don't. I already got it from Sam."

"Just swear to me you're not going to confront a murderer."

A smile crossed my lips. "I swear. It's someone who might have important information."

"Will they keep the rabbit?" He looked around. "Where is it, anyway?"

"Up in my room, sleeping. He should be fine." To be honest, I didn't know how long rabbits normally slept, but Kevin didn't need to know that.

Two minutes later, I was in my car, headed to the vet's clinic. According to the internet, they were available twenty-four hours a day. My maps app made it look like the veterinarian operated out of her house, which made sense since Third Street didn't have a ton of businesses.

The building was dark when I arrived, but a light was on in the front room of the attached one-story house. I couldn't see through the curtains, but had no reason to believe anyone else would be living here.

I knocked loudly, firmly. What I thought of as my "police officer" knock. Whether it worked or she thought I was out here with a sick animal didn't matter. The door opened.

She blinked repeatedly when she saw me. "Aly! Are the animals okay?"

"I don't know, *Mallory*." I said.

Her face went pale. "You should probably come in."

Although a voice in the back of my head strongly suggested I avoid being alone in a small, enclosed space with someone acting extremely suspicious, I didn't get a dangerous vibe off of her. Just a weird one.

To the left of the foyer was a small sitting room. A lamp shining on a side table must have been what I saw from outside. The room contained a cozy-looking gray sofa, a large bookcase along one wall, a television on the other, and a couple dozen figurines of dogs and cats crammed onto every available surface: the coffee tables, end tables, the mantel under the television, the windowsill.

She sat on the couch and gestured for me to do the same. I crossed my arms over my chest. "No, thanks, I'll stand. Why did you lie to me?"

"I didn't lie, exactly," she said. "Just left out some information."

"That's what we normally would call a *lie*," I said. "Also, you're using a fake name."

"I'm actually not. I got married after the wedding. Mr. Younger lives in Boston, so I gave you a legitimate Boston phone number. It just goes to a disposable phone."

"Why go to all the trouble? What do you want from me?"

"Listen, I know you're mad, but honestly, I meant well. When I got your email about Priscilla and Mary, it scared me. If those two know that you're on to them—you could be in real danger."

I shrugged. "Say I am in danger. How was pretending to be the town vet going to protect me?"

"I wasn't completely pretending. I am a veterinarian. This space was vacant, so I took advantage of the cover. I have been seeing patients for the past few weeks."

"Why?"

"Hold on a second." She turned toward the back of the house. "I'll be right back."

Since it seemed clear she didn't want me to go with her, for a minute I considered doing just that. But as long as she didn't return with a gun, I'd be okay.

Old habits died hard. As soon as Mallory disappeared, I wasted no time picking up the nearest cat figurine. It was about six inches long, with carefully sculpted light gray fur and a flat face. A Persian, I thought. How did a person use a cat figurine? I attempted petting it but just felt silly. Never mind.

Moving on, I picked up the nearest book on the shelf and paged through it, hoping to trigger something. Nope. This loss of my powers made me want to kick the carpet. Sure, my visions alerted me to the fact that Thelma stole her Daytime Emmy award, but they'd desert me when I needed to know something useful?

Footsteps down the hall alerted me to Mallory's return, so I hastily put the book back on the shelf. In her hands she held a crystal ball, similar to the ones Amira sold in the magic shop. About three inches in diameter, with some swirling colors inside. However, unlike the balls for sale at I'll Put a Spell on You, this one was glowing, as if lightning shimmered beneath the surface.

"What's that?" I asked. It didn't appear to be a weapon, but it was clearly magical.

"Katrina gave it to me," she replied. "She asked me to keep it safe until the time was right. I don't even know if I *believed* in it. But it didn't seem worth taking chances. And I'm pretty sure the time is right now."

"You're here to help us? How?"

She nodded. "I can't stay forever, unfortunately. I'm only renting this place for a month. But I've been waiting and watching, trying to figure out the right time to give it to you. Apparently that's now. Since you know who I am, there's no reason for me to stick around."

"May I?" I reached out my hands, and she placed the crystal ball into them. It felt warm to the touch, but not unpleasantly so. The lightning on the surface didn't sting. It was almost like a massage. Instinctively, I knew I held a great deal of power. Stronger than anything I'd experienced. "Are you a witch?"

She shook her head. "No, I don't have any powers. Katrina made this."

My sister-in-law was so much more than I ever guessed. I turned it over and over in my hands, completely in awe. "What does it do?"

"It contains a protection spell. About three months before she died, Katrina brought it to me. She needed someone she could trust with her life." Mallory swallowed. "And Kyle's. I don't know if she knew what would happen, but she gave me this to protect her son. It works better at closer range, so as soon as Christie told me you were asking questions about Mary and

Priscilla, I moved to Shady Grove and waited. You were never supposed to know I was here. I was fairly confident that Kevin's fur allergy would keep you three from getting a pet."

So much information in such a short time. I filtered through it as quickly as I could. "You're protecting Kyle?"

"Not me, Katrina. I'm just her intermediary."

A ridiculous thought raised its hopeful head inside me. "Have you talked to her since…?"

"I wish, but no. I can't communicate with dead people. I'm just a regular person with a magical object, trying to do some good for an old friend. But it's time for me to go home."

"That's it? You can't tell me anything else?" So many questions swirled through my head, I barely knew where to start. "Shouldn't this belong to Kevin?"

"I'm trusting you to pass it along. It feels right." She nodded toward my hands. "Mary and Priscilla shouldn't be able to hurt Kyle while you or Kevin have it. Not with magic, anyway."

"Do you know the range? Does it have to be near him to work?"

Mallory shook her head. "No idea. When she handed me the orb, she said if Kevin asked, tell him 'the mirror will reveal all.' I'm sorry, I don't know what that means. I hope he does."

When Kevin and Katrina lived in their McMansion, she had a large, fancy mirror hanging in the front hallway. According to my brother, she'd loved that mirror. It had originally hung in the entry of the new house, but Kevin moved it so it wouldn't get broken after Kyle learned to play ball. When I'd found it under his bed, I'd used it to scry a vision of her death.

The mirror told me some things, but not anything about the orb. Darn it. I'd have to talk to Kevin.

Tears filled my eyes. Here I'd worried that Mallory wanted to interfere, to hurt me. Instead, she'd given me the most amazing gift imaginable. "Thank you. I don't know how to repay you for this."

Our eyes met, and I felt the weight of each word. Katrina died to protect her son. She knew someone or something was after him, although she probably never imagined who it would be. And now, Kevin and I could protect him, too.

"Just keep that little boy safe," Mallory said. "He was Katrina's whole world. Don't let her sacrifice be in vain."

CHAPTER TWENTY-TWO

ALTHOUGH MY FIRST instinct when anything magical happened was to go straight to Olive, it was late when I left Mallory's house. Sam had gotten my "I'm alive" text but was waiting for an actual call. So was Kevin. Besides, I wanted to look into Katrina's mirror as soon as possible. There was a better chance I'd get answers there.

Kevin was skeptical at first, but when I pulled out the orb, his derision died on his lips. In a hushed tone, he said, "Can I touch it?"

"Yeah, sure. You believe me?"

"I do." He reached out and took the orb, weighing it in his hands. "I don't know how to explain this, but it feels like her. Like Katrina."

A smile spread slowly across my face. "Yeah. Yeah, that's exactly right. So what do we do with it?"

"First, I'm going to have a conversation with Mallory myself," he said. "As soon as we get our powers back. Until then... let's go look at this mirror."

Quietly we went upstairs and dragged the heavy wooden frame out from under Kevin's bed. Although the mirror was dustier than it had been six months, I didn't notice anything special about it. A once-highly polished surface. Carved mahogany frame. Together, we leaned it against the wall by the bedroom door. Then Kevin grabbed a towel from the linen closet to dust the surface.

"What do we do now?" I asked.

"Your guess is as good as mine." Kevin gazed at his reflection. "Mirror, mirror on the wall. Who is the fairest of them all?"

Nothing happened.

"Next you'll be saying Candyman three times," I said.

"What do you expect?" Kevin said. "My power is with lies. Unless someone appears in the mirror to talk to me, there's not a lot I can do."

"Katrina?" I called into the mirror, touching the surface. All I saw was my own face.

"Do you think she meant that you should scry the mirror?" Kevin asked.

I thought about that for a minute. "Katrina never knew about my powers. You can't scry. Can Mom?"

"Not to my knowledge."

"Which means, if she can, Katrina wouldn't have known." Thoughtfully, I tapped one finger against my lips while considering the mirror.

"What are you thinking?" Kevin said.

"I wonder if we're trying too hard," I said. "Imagine someone without any powers was looking for information."

"If you wanted to put a message in a mirror, what would you do?"

"Write on it in milk?" I said helplessly.

No, that would never work. The first time someone cleaned the mirror, my work would vanish.

"Now you're thinking like a scientist. Let's take that a step further."

"You want to form a hypothesis?"

"Yes, but what I'm suggesting is that we consider Occam's razor," Kevin said.

"The simplest explanation is usually the best?"

"Exactly." He picked up the mirror and turned it around. Protective brown paper covered the back of the glass. "There's more than one way to hide a message in a mirror. Do you have scissors?"

Of course.

Quickly I moved to the attached master bathroom and pulled a pair of nail scissors from a drawer in the vanity. They were small, but should do the trick. Holding them in one hand, I shoved the point into the back of the paper. It made a small hole. I raised the scissors to try again, but Kevin stopped me.

"Here." Stepping forward, he stuck one pinky into the circle left by the tiny blade and pulled. The paper came away easily, revealing the back of the mirror.

In the center, someone had taped a small envelope. The word "Kevin" was written in handwriting I recognized, but hadn't seen in years.

Tears came to my brother's eyes. I touched his arm. "Do you want to be alone while you read that?"

"No." He sniffled and squeezed my hand. "We've come this far together."

Slowly, almost reverently, he loosened the tape around the envelope and took it to sit on the bed. Then he took the nail scissors and used them to slit together.

After clearing his throat, he removed a single sheet of paper and began to read.

My dearest Kevin,

If you're reading this, I fear the worst has happened. Something is coming for me. Priscilla has sensed a powerful enemy in our future. Kyle is in danger. They want him for a spell. We have to protect him. I don't know the details, but I made an orb and put my essence in it. Since you found this letter, Mallory must have given it to you. If I fail to protect him, the orb may be the only way to keep him safe. Keep it nearby.

I love the two of you more than anything. Take care of each other.

All my love,
Katrina

IN SOME WAYS, the note raised more questions than it answered. Sure, it was great to know that the orb really was from my sister-in-law. Mallory hadn't tricked me or sent this to harm us. But also, every time I thought I got a handle on the Towne cousins, someone gave me new information. If Priscilla was trying to help Katrina, why didn't Priscilla tell her cousin who the "powerful enemy" was? Maybe if Katrina had known that her sister was the one to avoid, she'd still be here.

What kind of spell was Mary doing with Kyle, anyway? He was only a child. If this spell required a child's blood, she'd perform it over my dead body. Why were Priscilla and Mary together? Was Priscilla trying to keep her cousin in check?

A tear falling on the bottom of the page distracted me from those thoughts. Kevin quickly blotted it before it could smear the ink.

"It looks like Mallory was telling the truth," I said quietly. "If only Priscilla had told her where the danger was coming from."

"Yeah." He stared into the distance for a few minutes, blinking rapidly. I sat with him, not knowing what to say.

Finally, he set the letter on his nightstand. "I think I need to be alone."

"I get it. We'll talk in the morning." I stood to go. Halfway to the bedroom door, a thought occurred to me. "What do we do with the orb? Put it in your safe at work?"

"Yeah, for now. Unless you want to take it to Olive."

"I do. Tomorrow." With a big yawn, I stretched and held my hand out to take the orb back. "For now, bed."

Kevin met my gaze as he handed it over. "Tell me the truth, Aly. Do you think Katrina died because of me and Kyle—because I wanted a family?"

"No. She died because a bad person killed her. It's not your fault. Never your fault."

CHAPTER TWENTY-THREE

THE NEXT DAY, I woke up still amazed at the turn my investigation into Katrina's death had taken. I knew that Mary or Priscilla had killed Katrina, I knew it had something to do with Kyle's powers—but more importantly, now I knew Kevin and I could protect him. They couldn't come anywhere near my nephew.

The existence of the orb explained why the killer didn't take Kyle when she had the chance. It explained why Mary sent him a cursed rocking horse through me instead of bringing it to him personally. Funny how a few answers made the whole world look brighter. Yes, we still needed to catch the killer and bring her to justice. But we were making progress.

Speaking of progress, Jeff had been missing for almost a full seventy-two hours, and I was no closer to finding him than when he vanished. What did I know? Rainbow wanted his space, Whitney wanted his space—or at least, didn't want Jeff to have it—and the permit applications had gone missing. Jeff owed a lot of people money, including Mellie and his sister. Tory had money, or her husband did, but she didn't want Jeff to touch it.

Also, my stomach was growling. Maybe it was time to call in

the professionals. I wasn't a detective. I was a college junior who worked part-time in an antique store. When I'd helped police in the past, I'd used my visions to give me information. Without that possibility, I didn't have any useful skills. Just a newspaper article telling the people of Shady Grove not to trust me.

With a heavy sigh, I threw back the covers and got into the shower. Later, I'd text Doug the whole story and let them deal with everything. It was time for me to focus on something I could fix: getting my powers back.

First, I needed to get to Missing Pieces to show Olive the orb. Even without her powers, she knew things. She might be able to give me some idea where it came from, verify Mallory's story. Then she could help me research how these crystal balls were supposed to work.

Kyle knocked on my door as I finished getting dressed. "Aunt Aly! I need pancakes."

I ran a comb through my hair. When I didn't manage to wake up before Kyle, it usually had to air dry. "Aren't you sleeping? Maybe you should go back to bed."

"No!" He giggled. "I'm going downstairs."

"Use your manners."

"Please?"

I pretended to think for a minute. "Can Kelvy make your pancakes? I hear bunnies make the best pancakes."

"No!" He ran to the edge of the bed and tugged me to my feet. "Come on!"

After slipping my feet into slippers, I smoothed my hair again and grabbed a headband on the way out the bedroom door. It was my turn to make breakfast, and a plate full of pancakes did sound pretty good. Rolled pancakes with choco-late hazelnut spread were my weakness.

In the kitchen, Kyle and I worked together. We'd established a pretty good routine over the past year. Using a recipe found online, I measured the ingredients and put them in tiny bowls—

something I'd thought ridiculous when I'd first seen people doing it on Food Network. But with Kyle, it made perfect sense. He would stand on his stool by the kitchen counter and add the ingredients one by one, then whisk them all together. I'd pour batter onto the electric griddle and he'd watch for bubbles to appear on the surface. Three minutes later, through the glorious magic of teamwork, our breakfast would be ready. There would even be enough for Kevin if he got up before Kyle ate them all.

When I turned to set the maple syrup on the table, I almost dropped it. Lost in thought, I hadn't even seen Kyle going for the rabbit hutch until he'd opened it. Now, the gray and white creature stood on the edge of the table, nibbling a pancake.

"Kyle! Bunnies don't eat people food."

"What do they eat?"

"They eat rabbit food."

The expression my nephew gave me seemed way beyond his four years. It clearly said, "I know you don't know what you're talking about."

"I'm serious! We've got some from the vet in the pantry. I'll grab it. But you've got to move Kelvy. Your dad will flip if he finds an animal on the table."

As if he heard me, the rabbit lifted his head, a strip of pancake hanging from his mouth. I went to take it away from him, but he turned and hopped to the floor, dragging his prize behind him. At least he wasn't leaving a streak of chocolate hazelnut spread on the kitchen floor.

I started after him, but he'd already disappeared around the corner into the dining room. By the time I found him cowering between the hutch and the wall, the pancake had vanished. He met my gaze so steadily, it was a bit unnerving.

"Please don't bite me."

The rabbit obviously didn't respond, but inched out of his hiding place. I moved my hand as slowly as possible while he came closer. Finally, about fifteen years later, I managed to pick him up and deposit him back into the hutch.

The rabbit moved into the corner, stood up, and peeked out the roof of his cage. His nose wiggled furiously. Gazing at the pancakes, he started clucking.

"The bunny likes pancakes," Kyle said.

Upstairs, running water told me that Kevin had woken up and gotten in the shower. The clucking grew louder. He'd never know what the rabbit ate for breakfast.

"Okay, fine," I said. "But you better eat fast."

Quickly, before my better judgment could kick in, I grabbed the smallest remaining pancake and dropped it into the hutch. Kelvy settled onto it and began munching. If I didn't know better, I'd have sworn he was smiling.

Life in Shady Grove just kept getting more bizarre.

When I arrived at work half an hour later, Olive was searching around under the register. She stood up at the sight of me. "You're early. Couldn't sleep?"

"Not really." I pulled the orb out of my pocket.

Her mouth dropped open. "Where did you get that?"

"One of Katrina's bridesmaids gave it to me. She said it's supposed to be for protection." Quickly I explained what happened the night before. "I thought maybe you could test it, tell me more. Can you tell me if it really belonged to Katrina?"

She shook her head. "Probably not. My power generally doesn't work with magical objects. Even if it did, it sounds like that orb belongs to you now."

"That's what I thought. Will you still try it once your powers come back?"

"Of course I will," she said. "At the moment, all I can do is confirm that it's magical."

I snorted. "Thanks. The unearthly glow definitely didn't tell me that."

"That's a fine thank you," she said, but I could tell she wasn't really upset. "Have you considered asking Amira?"

To be honest, I hadn't because the orb was supposed to protect Kyle, and I hesitated at bringing anyone else into our circle of trust. Also, I'd been avoiding her ever since Kyle found Lola. There was no reasonable explanation and she clearly hadn't bought my lies. I liked Amira, and she'd helped me in the past—but I was extraordinarily protective of my nephew.

"You don't have to tell her that you're asking because of Kyle, do you?" Olive asked, correctly interpreting my silence.

"I suppose not," I said. "At a minimum, she could tell me whether the thing has been cursed, right?"

"Exactly."

"Do you think Amira's magic is on the fritz, like ours?" She was a witch, not a psychic, but without knowing what caused the problem, the entire town could be affected.

"Only one way to find out." Olive glanced at the clock. "You don't start for another forty-five minutes. Go."

When I'd first moved to town, I'll Put a Spell on You was open such random hours, people joked about it being a front of the mob. In reality. Mr. and Mrs. Patel were running it by appointment only while Amira took a sabbatical traveling around the world. Now, Amira typically opened at nine, which meant she should be working already.

After I thanked Olive, I put the orb back in my pocket and braced myself for the blast of humidity.

When I pushed on the front door of the shop, I discovered it still locked, but Amira moved around inside. I knocked, hoping she'd take a minute to come over and not make me come back later.

As soon as she saw me, Amira's eyes lit up. She dashed to the door, unlocking it so fast I worried she'd smack herself in the face with it.

"Aly, I'm so glad you dropped by!"

"Hey," I said. "How are you?"

"I am amazing!" She gripped both my hands in hers. "You saw my text? I found Lola! Thank you, thank you, thank you!"

"I'm so glad to hear that," I said. "Is she okay?"

"A little shaken up, but safe and sound. We think she went

in while Mr. Chang was mowing his lawn before he left. Said there was an issue with the lawnmower, and he spent a while tinkering with it. Anyway, she's sleeping at home now, happy as can be. I can't possibly thank you enough." She paused, studying me carefully. "Or Kyle."

I laughed nervously. "Kyle? He didn't have anything to do with it." My voice grew higher with each word until I had to stop talking or only dogs would be able to hear me. I was the worst liar.

"That's hogwash." Amira snorted. "Luckily, I'm too happy to have my little girl back to care. You need anything, it's yours."

"Funny you should mention that," I began. Then I realized how that sounded. "Wait. No. You don't actually owe me anything. But, I did come to ask a favor. How's your knowledge of magical objects?"

"Is the object itself magical or did someone put a spell on it?"

Her question immediately put me at ease. "Someone put a spell on it. Would you be able to tell me who did it? Or what kind of spell?"

I pulled out the orb, and she flinched. "Wow. You know some people with power."

That actually didn't make me feel any better, because as far as I knew, of all the Towne women, the one with the most power was Mary. If Katrina had a lot of power, how much more did her sister have?

"Is it dangerous?" I asked.

Amira weighed the orb in her palm for a minute, closed her eyes, then felt it again. She put both hands over it, moved it from one hand to the other, and said some words under her breath that weren't English. Then her eyes popped open. "No, I don't think it is."

"Forgive me for asking but have you had any trouble with your magic lately?" She shot me a quizzical look. "It's not that I don't believe you. It's just that I've had some issues with my visions. I wonder if it's just me or something in the air."

Or on the ground. Something small with gray ears.

She shook her head. "No, I'm at full strength. Have you been overly stressed?"

"Not before I lost my powers. I am now."

"Valid. Still, you have college classes and a job and you're taking care of a small child and a long distance boyfriend. You might just need to rest."

A wry grin crossed my lips. "Great. My powers should be back in about four years."

"Touché. Whatever it is, I hope you figure it out soon," she said.

"Thanks. Me, too. And thanks for your help with the orb."

"If you can leave it with me, I can run some tests." At my obvious hesitation, she held up one hand. "Never mind. Tell you what, I'll ask around. Okay?"

That sounded much better. I thanked her and turned to head back to work. When I reached the door, she called me back.

"Oh, but Aly?"

"Yeah?"

"In the wrong hands, all magical objects are dangerous. That one is very powerful. Be careful with it."

CHAPTER TWENTY-FOUR

MY SHIFT still didn't start for almost half an hour, so after leaving Amira, I decided to make one more detour. So far, I'd talked to all but one person who was on Main Street during the earthquake. As much as I preferred to avoid him, it was time to confront TJ about his lies and find out what he knew.

A few minutes after leaving the magic shop, I found myself in front of a three-story brick office building on the other side of the police station. Floor Zero contained the directory, restrooms, and the re-election center for Mayor Banister. I didn't even make eye contact with anyone there on my way to the staircase. Up on Floor One, I found a small literary agency, a realtor's office, and an insurance agency. Nothing to see there, either.

Finally, I reached the third floor, inexplicably named "Floor Two". The *Shady Grove Sentinel* offices didn't look much like I pictured. Maybe I watched too much *Supergirl,* but this was no massive office on top of a skyscraper with sweeping views. No sea of desks. Just a small room upstairs from an accountant's office with a landline, a couple of computers, and the office of Hal Crews.

Hal had run the *Shady Grove Gazette* for about ten years back when it was the *Shady Grove Beat,* and his dad did it before him.

He must've been disappointed when his only son decided to attend Maloney college, a small science-focused school.

Of course, you didn't need a degree when your family owned the paper.

A woman with her white hair pulled back into a bun and deep wrinkles greeted me when I walked in. She looked like your stereotypical librarian, which seemed appropriate. According to the gossip mill, Ethel had been Hal's father's receptionist for thirty years, then stayed on after he retired. She told everyone that she fully intended to work for TJ when he took over.

"Can I help you, dear?" she asked when I approached.

"Is TJ here?"

She waved one hand around the room. "If he is, I don't see him."

"Do you know where he is?"

"Why do you ask?" she said.

"I have some questions about an article he wrote," I said vaguely, unsure whether this sweet-looking woman was the enemy. Would she apologize and offer me cookies or throw me out for saying anything negative about darling little TJ?

She narrowed her eyes at me. "Hold on. Aluminum Reynolds?"

"It's Aly," I said automatically.

"TJ is unavailable."

"He doesn't want to talk to the person he wrote a hit piece on? What a shocker. Is his father around?"

"I'm afraid not. You'll have to write a letter to the editor."

Right. Send a letter to the editor, which would get opened by this woman and then tossed in the trash. "I'm here to demand he print a retraction."

She clucked her head and shook her head. "And what if we don't? Will you destroy this place, just like the pet store?"

"No, I'll call my brother the lawyer and ask him to sue the newspaper."

"It's not a lawsuit when it's the truth."

"You have absolutely no evidence that I had anything to do with the pet store incident, or Professor Zimm's death, for that matter. I caught the murderer!"

She arched one eyebrow. "Or did you? Anyway, I'd love to help, but I can't. TJ didn't say anything bad about you in that article. He relayed the facts and allowed people to draw their own conclusions."

Sometimes I wished my powers gave me the ability to freak people out by making steam flow from my ears. Since it didn't, there was no point in continuing this conversation. As Ethel pointed out, TJ wasn't here, and his dad wasn't, either. I was wasting my time.

I spun on my heel and strode for the door, hoping to make a dramatic exit. As I reached to throw the door open before stomping out, it moved away from me. I stopped in my tracks at the site of Hal. He looked like a time-lapsed photo of TJ, except he'd allowed his red hair to grow into a fiery halo of curls around his face.

"Good afternoon," he said with a big smile. "How can I help you?"

The greeting disarmed me, as it was probably meant to do. Ethel had been all smiles, too, until she heard why I was there.

I paused. "I'm Aly Reynolds."

Hal nodded sagely. "I had a feeling you'd be coming around. Please, come to my office."

Ethel let out a sound of outrage, which Hal ignored. I turned around and smirked at her before following Hal to the back of the room, through a small door I hadn't noticed earlier. Every square inch of the office beyond that door was covered in paper. The desk, the floors, even the chair where Hal invited me to sit. I picked them up, holding several pages uncertainly while I perched on the edge of my seat. If this man talked to me the way his receptionist did, I could be out that door in mere seconds. As long as I didn't trip.

I started to put the papers on the desk when the words on the top one caught my eye. *Dear Editor, I am writing about the piece your son wrote on my poor cat, Fluffy, digging up my neighbor's garden.*

Hal cleared his throat, so I guiltily put the pages on the edge of the overflowing desk, but not before the name at the bottom caught my eye. Mrs. Chang. I apparently wasn't the only one upset at the way TJ took liberties with the truth.

I opened my mouth to apologize, but Hal beat me to the punch. "I'm sorry for my son, Aly. That piece he wrote on you was unfair, biased, and unforgivable. I will be printing a retraction tomorrow."

"How did it get printed in the first place?"

He tugged at his ear, then wiped his nose nervously before folding his hands on the desk and looking me in the eye. "He snuck it in. I had to leave early yesterday for an appointment, so I asked TJ to finish the layout and take the pages to the printer. He's done it before. It never occurred to me that he would change the front page."

"I still don't understand why," I said.

"I'm going to level with you. My boy isn't thrilled to be working at the *Shady Grove Sentinel*. 'Such a boring town,' he says. 'Nothing interesting ever happens here'. He thought when he graduated college he'd get a job at a high-paying think tank and win the Nobel Prize, not come back here to live with me."

To be honest, TJ wasn't entirely wrong. Shady Grove wasn't the most interesting place in the world, and I grew up in a suburb where the only thing to do before turning twenty-one was to sit around with friends and talk about how we wished for something to do. Still, that didn't mean he could make up news.

"What did he major in?" I asked.

"Biology. Physics. Chemistry. Geology. Botany."

My eyes widened. "He did five majors?"

"He did. Not all at once, though." Hal coughed. "Ultimately, he got his degree in anatomy, but doesn't want to go to medical school. I'm sorry to say, my son is a bit adrift right now. But that doesn't excuse his behavior. How can I make things right?"

"I would appreciate the retraction," I said.

"Done. Anything else?"

I thought for a minute. "Did you hear anything unusual about the earthquake that hit the other day?"

"An earthquake in these parts *is* unusual. We haven't had a disaster like that since a vat of maple syrup broke on Main Street back in the 1850s. Long before my time, I'm afraid." He shook his head sadly. "TJ wrote the story. Best one he's put out in a long time. We were both so upset when it didn't get picked up anywhere else."

"You mean the Associated Press?"

"Well them, sure. But we trade stories with the *Willow Falls Window* sometimes, and they turned us down flat. Said the quake hadn't been felt over there, so it must not have been a big deal." He sighed. "Couldn't get the TV stations on board, either. One guy accused us of making the whole thing up."

Emma hadn't felt the earthquake, and she was on the town line. It shouldn't have been a big surprise that the rest of Willow Falls hadn't noticed it. But it occurred to me that Mellie hadn't felt it over by the golf course, either. Thelma said she'd only heard about the quake from Amira. A tremor big enough to knock me flat and trash a couple of stores on Main Street should have carried for miles. That was big news, especially in upstate New York.

What was going on?

CHAPTER TWENTY-FIVE

ALL THE WAY back to Missing Pieces, I rolled the facts over in my mind. The earthquake no one felt outside of Shady Grove. The loss of our powers. The missing pet store owner. Business permit applications that vanished.

I had to be overlooking something obvious. My mind was a jumbled mess from learning to care for a new pet to worrying that my powers would never come back to hoping Jeff would miraculously appear, alive, and unharmed. I turned it over and over but couldn't make sense of it. There had to be a way to unravel things and put it all back together in a way that made sense.

Those thoughts fled when I got back to the store, entering through the employees' entrance. The coffee maker sat on the counter where I'd left it, still at the two cup line (which barely filled my mug one-third of the way). Beside it, someone had left a pair of men's black sunglasses and a pair of earbuds.

At the sight of those items, my spirits lifted considerably. I spun around, eyes searching for the owner.

"Sam?" I called.

No answer. Wheeling around, I ran for the front of the store. There he was, sitting at the bistro table sipping from one of

Julie's takeout cups. A second cup and a white paper bag sat on the table in front of him. His attention was focused on his mother, who stood in her usual spot behind the register.

"Sam!"

When I called his name, his head swiveled around. He was on his feet before I crossed the ten feet or so to the table. "Aly!"

I tackled-hugged him, squeezing with all my might. Leaning onto my tiptoes, I kissed him quickly. "This is so amazing! Why didn't you tell me you were coming?"

"I wanted to surprise you." He kissed the tip of my nose before pulling me into another hug. "From the look on your face, I'd say mission accomplished."

"Best. Mission. Ever. What about work?"

"I had a few vacation days saved. After our conversation last night, I needed to be here."

My cheeks grew warm, and I avoided his gaze. "It feels like I'm always counting on you to fix things for me."

Sam's fingers touched my chin. Gently, he brought my eyes back to meet his. "We're a team, Aly. I help you, you help me."

"How do I help you?"

"Just by being you." He kissed me again. I leaned into it, too happy about seeing him again to care that we had an audience.

Olive cleared her throat. "Not to break up the touching reunion, but Sam and I have been talking about what's been going on."

I pulled back, not embarrassed in the slightest. "Any ideas?"

"Mom and I have been talking, but nothing concrete," he said. "Still, three heads are better than two. What can you tell me?"

I walked Sam through everything that had happened since the earthquake. Olive pretended to cover her ears when I got to the part about breaking into Jeff's house, but didn't interrupt. Sam asked a couple of clarifying questions.

I finished up by telling them both about the experiments Kevin and I did, including the fact that Emma still had her powers and didn't feel the earthquake. Neither did anyone else in Willow Falls.

"I need my powers!" I clenched my fists in frustration and threw myself down on the second chair beside the table. "If I could just have a vision, everything would make sense."

"You say that now," Olive said with a knowing smile. In truth, many of my visions had given me more questions than answers.

But some answered things!

Taking a deep breath, I resisted the urge to bang my head against the table. If the visions couldn't tell me what happened, I'd just have to find out the truth some other way.

"We can figure this out," I said decisively. "Sam, grab me the chalkboard from the back corner?"

He looked around the store as if seeing it for the first time. "Mom has a chalkboard in here?"

"Well, it's a child's easel, but yes. It's for sale. It's also portable."

"On it!"

"What are you planning to do?" Olive asked. "Draw a chalk circle for protection to break the spell?"

I shook my head. "No. I'm going to reason this through. Our magic isn't working, but before I found my magic, I was a scientist. Logic and reasoning never let me down."

She smiled serenely. "Except when the answer is 'magic'."

I huffed. "I knew you'd say something like that."

Before she could reply, Sam returned with the easel, setting it down to face the register. The board had a few random markings on it from shoppers, so I scrubbed it clean before lifting a piece of chalk. Meanwhile, Sam settled at the bistro table near the front register. From where Olive sat, both of them could easily view my writings.

"Where do we start?" Sam asked.

"At the beginning, right?" It seemed reasonable, even if it made that song from *Sound of Music* get stuck in my head. I drew two lines down the center. "Here is Main Street. This is I'll Put a Spell on You, Missing Pieces, and On What Grounds?." As I spoke, I chalked in the different places, along with Town Square at the end of the street.

I continued. "At approximately nine-fifteen on Saturday morning, Kyle and I arrived at the pet store." I put a big "A" and a little "k" on the board to mark our spots. "By then, Jeff was gone. Amira was approaching from the other direction, but she never entered the store."

An "AP" noted the spot where we'd run into her.

"You didn't see her go inside," Olive said. "Do you know where she was before the quake?"

Hmm. Amira said she hadn't gone in, and she'd been walking up, but the shop had a back door. She theoretically could have gone in, kidnapped Jeff, left through the back and… what? Hidden him in her pockets? The lack of clues was making me lose my mind. Amira was a talented witch, but not even she could make a grown man disappear. Nor did she have any conceivable reason to do that.

"She came from the other end of Main Street, so possibly from home unless she got breakfast at Patti's Diner," I said.

"Where was Kevin?" Olive asked.

Another two lines on the board indicated Second Street, with Kevin's office, not far from Missing Pieces. Then I put a big "K" where he worked, and for good measure added an "O" on the board to represent Olive.

"Stop." Sam said.

"What? You think your mother did it?"

"No, of course not. But do you see what I see?"

I looked from the board to my boyfriend and back several times. "All I've done is plot where everyone was when the earthquake hit the town."

"Exactly." He stood up and approached the board. Taking a pink piece of chalk, Sam circled the "A" and "k", then circled the "K" for Kevin. He drew a straight line from one to the next.

It passed neatly through the box representing Missing Pieces. "You and Kevin were affected, as was the person standing between you—Mom. Amira is fine, and she was approaching from the other end of Main Street."

"What about Kyle? He was with me. Right after the earthquake, Kyle helped Amira find her lost dog." The fact that Kyle wasn't affected was why I didn't seriously consider the earthquake as related to our power loss.

Olive thought for a minute. "That is interesting. Someone did a spell, which created an earthquake and took your powers, plus Kevin's. It also affected me because I was in the linear path between you. Kyle was also with you, but unharmed. Is that right?"

I nodded. The answer came to me right as she opened her mouth to speak. "The orb!"

"It must have protected him," Olive said.

"Glad to know it works, at least." I said.

"That means we pull Kyle out of the equation," Sam said. "When you look at the board, what do you see?"

My mouth dropped open. "You don't think anyone was after Jeff at all. He was collateral damage."

"That's exactly what I think," Sam said.

"We've gotten it all backwards," I said. "This whole time, we were trying to figure out who would want to hurt Jeff."

"—when the real question was, who wants to hurt you and Kevin?" Olive said. "We all know the answer to that."

Only one person benefitted from taking my powers, Kevin's, and Olive's at the same time. That same person wouldn't care who got hurt in the process: Katrina's killer.

"Poor Jeff," I moaned as I sank onto the bistro chair and dropped my head into his hands. "He's gone missing and it's all my fault. He could even be dead!"

"Stop," Sam said, rubbing my back. "You're not responsible for anyone else's actions. This is no one's fault except the killer's."

Olive stepped forward. "But who *is* the killer? Was it Priscilla or Mary?"

That was the million-dollar question. My vision hadn't told me. None of the evidence we'd uncovered seemed helpful at first. But now, after hearing about the magical attack on Mallory, everything came together. The magical rocking chair that hurt Olive. Mary's own admission that she was a witch. The way Priscilla sensed I'd be visiting her at Destiny's Haven. Kevin's belief that Priscilla got feelings but couldn't do magic. As all the pieces fell into place, I felt the answer in my bones.

"It's Mary. Priscilla's a psychic, like me. Mary's the witch."

CHAPTER TWENTY-SIX

WE DIDN'T HAVE any time to spare. If Mary did a spell to divest me and Kevin of our powers—not caring who else might be affected—she wasn't going to hang around while we figured out how to get them back. And if she had enough power to nearly bring down an entire pet store, she needed to be stopped as soon as possible.

It had been three days since the earthquake. I didn't know how long that orb would hold Mary at bay. It was supposed to protect Kyle from magic—but what if someone came at him with a gun? I didn't want to find out.

"Olive?" I asked. "This kind of spell. How near would a person have to be to the subjects to perform it?"

Her eyes widened. "Call Kevin. Sam, go get Amira."

He was on his feet and at the door practically before I found my phone and tapped my brother's name. I didn't bother with preamble when he answered. "Get Kyle. Get out of town now."

"Aly? What are you talking about?"

"Our lost powers aren't because of Jeff's disappearance. Jeff is missing because Mary magically attacked us when I was standing outside his store. I don't know what happened to him, but her spell caused the earthquake. It made him vanish. Mary wants us defenseless. My guess is that only the orb has kept her from swooping in to take him."

"Are you sure?"

"I'm sure. Is Kyle with you?"

"No, he's with Mrs. Patel. She took him to the park."

Amira's mother. Who wouldn't have been anywhere near Main Street when the spell hit. Kevin and I inherited our powers from our mother; Kyle got his from both parents. Everything clicked into place.

"Is Mrs. Patel a witch?" I was already moving toward the door. Olive called my name, but I ignored her.

He made an exaggerated "hmm" sound. "You know, now that you mention it, I think she might be."

"Kevin! You knew and you never told me?"

"To be fair, you waited months to tell me about your powers," he said. "But I wouldn't trust Kyle to just anyone. Not after what happened to Katrina."

For the first time in more than a day, I breathed a sigh of relief. Between Mrs. Patel and the orb providing magical protection, Kyle was going to be okay. We'd find him, get him in a secure location, then get our powers back. I increased my pace to Olympic speed walker. "What's the next step?"

"I'm getting in my car now. Hold on." A door slammed, the line paused, and when he spoke again, his voice was farther away, letting me know the Bluetooth had picked up the conversation. "I'm driving to the park to get them. Where are you?"

"I just left Missing Pieces. Sam was going to get Amira and come back. I'll head them off. But I don't know where to go. Our house isn't safe, is it?"

"The protection spells Mrs. Patel established when we moved in should still be in place. Kyle is supposed to be safe when he's there. I suspect the orb will give those spells a boost if you bring it back. The fact that no one has entered in the past three days makes me think our house should be reasonably safe."

"Great." I came to a halt. "What if Priscilla shows up?"

"She can't be up to any good. At this point, if you see either of them, let me know."

"Good point." Neither of the Towne cousins had a valid reason for being in Shady Grove. We had reasons to distrust both, even if only Mary had the power to pull off a spell of this magnitude. Especially when it seemed so likely they were in cahoots.

Ahead of me, Sam and Amira exited the magic shop. I waved them toward me as I told Kevin I'd see him at home and hung up. It only took a minute to fill them in on our conversation.

"Mom and I have both been researching how a person can lose their powers," Amira said. "When I talked to her this morning, she was almost ready to do a reversal spell."

"Do you know what we'll need?" Sam asked.

"I think so. Let me grab a few supplies. I'll meet you at your house." Amira wheeled around and headed for I'll Put a Spell on You.

Sam put one hand on my shoulder. "It's going to be okay, Aly. We'll make sure no one hurts Kyle."

His words, as always, relaxed me. Not for the first time, I wondered if my boyfriend was some kind of empath. He always seemed to know when I needed to calm down. I took a second to breathe deeply. "We can't lose him, Sam."

"We won't." He kissed me softly. I took strength from him, and when we parted, my heart and soul both felt better. "Come on. Let's go to your house."

"Not yet. We need your mom. If Mrs. Patel is going to reverse the spell, she should be there, too."

"Do you want me to wait at the store?"

I shook my head. I'd feel much better with Sam by my side. "No. I want you with me."

Fifteen minutes later, I sat at the dining room table with Kevin, Mrs. Patel, Olive, and Amira. As soon as we arrived,

Sam took Kyle into the living room to watch cartoons. We wanted him close enough to keep an eye on him, but he didn't need to see or hear everything.

Kyle protested at first, since he could tell the grown-ups were doing something important. But in the end, the lure of the television was too strong. He asked Sam to move the hutch to the coffee table so Kelvy could enjoy the cartoons, and all three of them left the room.

"What exactly are you going to do?" I kept my voice down as Amira set candles in a circle around the table. The doorway between the dining room and living room was fairly open.

"It's a binding spell," Mrs. Patel began.

"Aren't we already bound?" I asked.

"Not us," Amira said. "The witch who did this. Our power replenishes itself when we rest, just like how drinking quenches thirst or sleeping gives you more energy. To continue keeping you from using your powers, the witch has to be using quite a bit of energy. Mom is going to target them, bind them, and drain them."

Impressive.

"Do you need to know where they are to do that?"

Mrs. Patel shook her head. "Often, it is helpful to be within striking distance of the witch. But I don't need to physically locate her when I know who it is."

My brows knit together as I turned her words over. "What if we're wrong? What if Priscilla is also able to cast spells?"

"We are fairly certain that the witch has the same maternal DNA as Kyle," Amira said. "You did experiments on that, right?"

"Mitochondrial DNA, yeah," I said. "Did Sam tell you about that?"

She nodded.

Kevin held up Kyle's hairbrush. "We can use this to find and bind both Mary and Priscilla, even if only one of them cast the spell."

"How long will the binding last?"

"Long enough. If this works, it'll take weeks for her to get back to full strength."

At Mrs. Patel's direction, I dimmed the lights while Amira lit the candles. Kevin opened a window, then Olive lit some incense. We all took our seats and held hands.

"Close your eyes," Mrs. Patel said. "Breathe deeply and count backward from ten. When we get to one, I'll begin."

We counted. With each breath, the smoke filled my lungs, leaving me more at ease. I didn't know what was in that incense, but by the time we got to one, I felt calm enough to fall asleep.

Mrs. Patel started speaking rapidly in a language I didn't understand. The rest of us remained silent. She clapped. I began to feel light-headed.

"So mote it be!" Mrs. Patel yelled. Then a moment later, she said, "Huh."

That didn't sound right.

Squinting, I opened one eye. Everything looked the same as before. Rather than asking whether the spell worked, I said, "Kevin, I love football."

"False," he said automatically. "But the spell didn't work."

Darn it.

I blinked back tears of disappointment. "What happened?"

"I don't think I have enough power," Mrs. Patel said. "Whoever cast this spell is stronger than me."

"Is there a way to counteract that?" I asked.

Olive said, "Another witch could add their powers to hers. Maybe Emma?"

I shook my head. "Emma's a hearth witch. She does spells related to house and home. I'm not sure if she could work something like this, but I can call her."

Amira bit her lip thoughtfully. "What we need is some kind of catalyst."

"Do you mean a magical object?" My eyes met Kevin's as I spoke.

He nodded slowly, then pulled the orb out of his pocket. It shone even brighter than before. "Something like this?"

Mrs. Patel studied my brother. "You've been holding out on me."

"I swear, I haven't," he said. "Aly and I just got this."

"Tell me about it later," she said, taking the orb.

"Hold on," I said. "Can you use that without taking its powers?"

She nodded as the orb went onto the table in front of her. "A catalyst will magnify the spell, but its powers remain the same. Everyone hold hands and close your eyes. We're doing this again. Count backwards from ten."

Amira lit another stick of incense, then settled back into her chair. We joined hands and closed our eyes. Like before, the counting and breathing relaxed me. Mrs. Patel started speaking again. This time, I recognized the language as the one she'd used before. No one else moved or spoke. I hardly dared to breathe for fear of messing something up.

"So mote it be!" Mrs. Patel said a second time. She clapped again.

Immediately, I opened my eyes. Everything felt different. The hairbrush floated about six inches off the table. Swirling lights danced around us like aurora borealis.

Something hovered in the air, that light, fizzy sensation I associated with using my powers. A wind spiraled overhead until it settled on my shoulders. Suddenly, I felt whole. Complete. Until that moment, I hadn't fully realized it, but I hadn't been my entire self.

"It's working!" Amira yelled. "I can feel it."

Something popped. The air filled with smoke. My eyes watered furiously, and a coughing fit racked my body. Wind tore through the room, blowing my hair back. Something screamed, but it wasn't any of us.

The smoke twirled around until it settled into a familiar face, hanging above the table. "You think you're so smart, don't you?"

"Give up, Mary," Kevin said. "It's over."

She cackled. "Oh, no. You don't know what you're dealing with. I'll see you soon."

"Be gone, witch!" Mrs. Patel yelled.

She flung her hands at the image. I felt rather than saw the power released. Mary let out another scream and then vanished.

A loud crack filled the air, followed by several small thuds.

Beyond the doorway, someone cried out. Kyle yelped.

Kevin and I shouted his name, practically in unison. I leapt to my feet, knocking the chair backward in my haste to get to the door.

My nephew's response was immediate. "I'm okay!"

"Don't move!" I called. "I'll find you."

I took three steps forward before the smoke dissipated.

"My bunny!" Kyle wailed.

Oh, no. My heart pounded.

"It's okay, buddy," Kevin said beside me. "Everything will be okay."

Not knowing whether my brother could see any better than me, I feared the worst. Did the explosion kill the rabbit? Then I blinked rapidly, and my eyesight finally cleared.

The coffee table lay in pieces on the ground, with what appeared to be a mangled hutch on top of it. As we'd feared, something terrible had happened to Kelvy. He'd vanished.

In his place, lying on our living room carpet, was Jeff Ahn.

CHAPTER TWENTY-SEVEN

JEFF AHN LAY on the floor of our living room. How was that possible? Did Mary send him?

No, that didn't make sense.

Element eighty-seven was francium. Element eighty-eight was radium. Elements eight-nine through one hundred three were in that pullout section at the bottom of the periodic table.

Focus, Aly.

For a long moment, no one spoke. Maybe they were all trying to regulate their breathing, too. Olive, Amira, and Mrs. Patel appeared in the doorway separating the living room from the dining room. They all looked as dumbstruck as I felt. Kevin stepped forward, placing himself between Jeff and Kyle in a neat move that looked almost choreographed. On the floor, Jeff gazed up at us like Dorothy at the end of *The Wizard of Oz.*

A thousand questions filled my mind at once, until they tripped over themselves on my tongue to get out. But one thing seemed clear. The rabbit was gone, and a man lay on our floor in his place. A fully clothed man, a small favor for which I felt very grateful at the moment. "Jeff! All along, that was you?"

He nodded. "I know it's hard to believe. Perhaps less so after what I've witnessed in the past twenty minutes or so."

"You're… a rabbit man?" I asked, knowing how it sounded but unable to stop myself.

He snorted. "Not exactly. I'm a witch. One of the things I've perfected over the years is how to transform into an animal. My first choice is the rabbit, because I like being able to jump."

"Where did the bunny go?" Kyle asked

Jeff addressed his question first with an indulgent smile. "I'm sorry to disappoint you, young man, but that bunny was me."

"But why? How? When? Why?" I asked.

"Very good questions," Jeff said. "If you would be so kind as to get me a glass of water, I'll explain everything. I'm parched."

"You took my bunny," Kyle said.

Jeff leaned down and tousled Kyle's hair. "I *am* your bunny. Thank you for taking such good care of me. I turned into a bunny because I was scared. Do you ever get scared?"

Kyle nodded. "Yeah. Daddy takes care of me. Your reading glasses are in your black jacket."

"Excuse me?" Jeff asked.

I paused on my way to the sink. Sure, Jeff had been living in our house as a bunny for several days and we'd fed and took care of him, but could we trust him with the secret of my nephew's powers? We didn't know whose side he was on.

Before I could react, Kyle said, "You lost your reading glasses. They're in your black jacket."

Jeff rubbed his chin thoughtfully. "You know, I think you're right. The last time I saw them was the day my animals were delivered to Paws and Effect. I had to go outside to direct the unloading, and a storm was brewing so I grabbed my raincoat. I put my glasses on to read the contract from the moving company. It makes sense that I would have stuffed them in my pocket when I took them off."

After filling up the glass of water, I returned and handed it to Jeff. As he gulped it down, I said, "Sometimes Kyle makes lucky guesses."

He winked at me. "Your secret is safe. After what you did for me, I owe you."

"It was nothing," I said. "All we did was take in a lost bunny who needed a home. What happened to you?"

Jeff drained the rest of the glass and set it on a coaster. "When the store started shaking, I didn't know what was happening. I thought someone had sent debt collectors after me. The magical kind. Immediately, I shifted into bunny shape so I could hide until the danger passed."

"Smart," I said.

"Not too smart. I got stuck."

"Stuck?"

"Yes. I should've known. The transformation was more difficult than usual, but I thought that was due to my fear. For whatever reason, I got stuck in rabbit form. I couldn't change back. Usually I'm only a rabbit for a couple of hours, max. I don't know what went wrong."

"It was Mary," Kevin said. "My former sister-in-law."

"Why would your sister-in-law curse me?" Jeff asked.

"It wasn't intentional," Kevin said. "You happened to be too close. Sorry about that, by the way. You were the victim of a plot intended for us."

"It's okay," Jeff said. "You're not the only one who should apologize."

My heart pounded at his words, instantly on the alert. "What are you talking about?"

"That reporter. He wrote the story about how trouble follows you wherever you go?"

Oh, fluorine. Not again.

"How did you know about that?" Kevin asked.

"It was lining the bottom of my cage."

"Don't tell me you believe TJ," I said.

"No, actually, I think it was my fault he singled you out," Jeff said. "Immediately after the quake ended, he came into the shop and started calling for me."

"How did you know him?"

Jeff's cheeks turned red. "He, ah, is dating my house cleaner's daughter. She must have mentioned that I owed them money. Which I'm going to pay immediately, I promise."

That reminded me. "Before you do, you should know she stole your Nintendo Switch."

He snorted. "Thanks. Anyway, when TJ came into the store, I'd already shifted. I didn't want to change back with him standing there, and at that point I didn't realize I'd gotten stuck. But then his phone rang. He started talking to someone, whining that it wasn't his fault nothing interesting ever happened in Shady Grove. Complained that he never got the big stories."

"He was talking to his dad at the paper," I said, remembering my conversation with Hal.

"I think so. Anyway, once he hung up, TJ started looking around. After a minute, he began tossing things around, making a huge mess."

So that's why the entire store was trashed, but the boxes stacked neatly in the back room remained in a perfect pile. I knew something seemed off about it.

"But why would he focus on Aly?" Olive asked.

"Because I showed up." I sighed heavily. I couldn't believe that, of all the theories Rainbow spewed to me and Rusty, this one actually had some basis in fact. We'd immediately discarded it as something she said because she didn't like the guy. "If we hadn't run into Amira outside, she would have gone in first. He would've blamed it on her."

"He must have heard you three talking, then skipped out the back door and went around to the front," Jeff said.

"Where did the blood come from? In the store."

"I got a nasty paper cut going through my mail," he said. "Hit the meaty part and it just wouldn't stop oozing. The shaking started while I was in the back looking for a bandage. I'm sorry it gave you such a scare."

"Don't be," I said. "You didn't do anything."

"You sure you don't want me to turn him into a rabbit for you?" Jeff's eyes danced, although I wasn't sure he could really do that.

"Don't tempt me," I said.

"Seriously, I do owe you. You and Kyle took good care of me. You even cleaned up the pet store and called Dr. Younger to keep an eye on my stock. No one asked you to do any of that."

Heat traveled up my neck to my cheeks. I dropped my gaze. "It was nothing. Anyone would've done it."

"TJ's behavior makes it clear that not *everyone* would have done the same thing," Jeff said. "You're something special."

"We all think so," Olive said.

"Listen, I've got to go check on my animals. I should call Dr. Younger and thank her for her time. Pay her for her services. But Kyle never got his pet. Please, come by the store tomorrow and I'll give him—"

"A goldfish, right?" Kevin cut in.

Jeff winked at me. "Sure thing. A goldfish. See you tomorrow, Aly."

"Bye, Jeff." A thought occurred to me. "Hold on."

"What?"

"Are you okay financially? I found a lot of bills." My cheeks grew warm when I realized everyone was still listening. "And your sister said you were asking for money."

"Ah," he said. "I understand. I'd been waiting on a small business loan that got delayed. Some of my contractors have been extremely patient with me. The check cleared yesterday before the earthquake, so I'll get right on that. Everything should be fine."

We all said goodbye. After engulfing everyone in a massive group hug, Jeff left. Taking his lead, Olive, Amira, and Mrs. Patel followed. Sam hung behind only for a minute to say goodbye to Kyle.

As I walked him to the front door, Sam looked back at my

brother before leaning toward me. He dropped his voice to a whisper. "Why do I think that little boy is about to get a magical puppy?"

"Thankfully, I don't think the pet shop sells such a thing." I grinned and shook my head as I closed the door behind him. The last thing this house needed was another magical inhabitant.

EPILOGUE

WITH THE ORB locked safely away in Kevin's office and our powers back in place, I finally managed to rest easily. Knowing we had an advantage over Mary took a huge load off my mind. When she showed up, we'd be ready.

Saturday morning while Kevin and Kyle enjoyed a birthday cartoon marathon, I snuck out of the house and back to Paws and Effect.

It didn't take long to find what I wanted. When I carried a glass aquarium into the living room, the two of them were still nestled together on the couch.

Upon seeing me, Kyle bolted upright. "What's that?"

"Not to alarm you," Kevin said, "but your goldfish doesn't have any water. And it seems to have four legs."

Grinning, I set the glass case gently on the floor because our new coffee table hadn't been delivered yet. "This is Mercury."

"Mercury!" Kyle came over and knelt on the ground, pressing his small nose against the glass. "Can I pet him?"

Kevin snickered at me. "You named a turtle Mercury?"

I shrugged. "Well, you know. It's a family tradition at this point."

Although we'd originally discussed a goldfish, after seeing

how Kyle helped me with Jeff-the-Rabbit all week, he'd seemed ready for something a little hardier. Neither Kevin nor I felt that a dog or cat would be appropriate considering how little we were home, but a turtle could be a good pet. For one thing, they lived roughly forty thousand times longer than a goldfish.

"Do you want to find Mercury a place in your room?" I asked Kyle. "I got you some books to read, and I'll show you how to feed him."

"Yaaaaaay." He raced for the stairs, off so fast I had to call him back to help carry everything.

Kyle's birthday party was a smashing success, largely because Kevin rented a bounce house. We'd invited all the kids from his preschool class, and they ate Julie's cupcakes then jumped until they could barely stand.

By the time everyone left, I was exhausted. Kyle wandered over, cake smeared on his face, a piece of paper in one hand.

"Looks like you had fun, huh?"

He nodded and held out the paper. "I made you a picture."

On the paper, he had made a few figures, clear enough that an adult may have assisted. First a tall person with spiky brown hair, standing beside a much shorter person with long brown hair. A third brown-haired figure stood beside us, this one holding what looked like a tiny green football.

"This is beautiful," I said sincerely. "Can you tell me about it?"

"I made our family." He ran away, with no idea how my heart swelled at those words. Such a special little boy.

Later that night, after dinner, Julie produced two grocery bags from the trunk of her car. First, we all enjoyed frosted sugar cookies shaped like bunnies. Then, when Kevin and I went to clean up, Julie took Kyle to the kitchen table to show him how to cut his own shapes.

Once the final bag of trash had been taken outside, Kevin and I sipped iced coffee at the island, watching the two of them.

"She's really good with him," I said.

He hmmed a non-reply.

"She fits in well with our family," I added.

"She does." He paused. "She's really special, Aly. I think this could turn into something."

The words brought a smile to my lips. "I'm so glad to hear that. I've been worried that you would never move on."

"Me, too. All this time, I've been holding back. But I want to move forward, with Julie. And I think I finally know how to do that."

I dropped my voice to a whisper, although Julie and Kyle were deeply engrossed in a discussion of whether he should make superhero cookies or animal shapes. "Kevin! Are you going to propose?"

His eyes danced. "Don't you think Julie should be the first to know the answer to that question?"

"Look, all I'm asking is if I need to buy something fancier than yoga pants."

He shook his head. "Not yet. There's something I have to do first."

That made me sit up straighter. "Did you figure out how to find Mary?"

"No, but I've been doing a lot of thinking. Researching the orb, talking to Amira. I even had an interesting conversation with Pink."

"You went to visit Emma without me?" Actually, that wasn't the strangest part of his sentence. "You learned how to talk to her cat?"

"Don't be ridiculous. Emma interpreted."

"Don't leave me hanging here. What did he say?"

"Pink suggested there's more to the orb than what we thought. That makes sense, since we used it for the spell." He picked up his mug in both hands and took a long swallow. "All this time, we've been trying to find Mary and/or Priscilla when we know they want to come to us. We've been moving in the wrong direction."

I didn't like where this conversation was going. "Please tell me you're not suggesting we use your four-year-old son as bait to catch a murderer."

He gave me a withering look. "Of course not. But I think we can do a spell, use the crystal ball to lay the trap. Kyle will be far away."

Realization dawned. "You're going to use the crystal ball to lay a trap for them. Create some kind of decoy Kyle?"

"Exactly. I'll ask Mom to come visit, take him to Boston for the weekend. You know she's been dying to show him the aquarium. Mrs. Patel can go with them. Once they're safely checked into their hotel, we'll start the spell."

A slow smile spread across my face. "And then we'll reel them in."

"That's right," he said. "It's time to end this thing, once and for all."

HOW

DOES

IT

END?

There's a killer on the loose, and they look like Aly.

Aly's used to getting visions by now, but she never expected to see herself murdering the town's beloved yet crotchety baker. She's completely baffled because, obviously, that never happened. Then police arrive at her house with a warrant. If she didn't kill Tony, why does she have his baker's hat?

When Aly finds herself reliving the same day over and over,

things go from strange to supernatural. Where did that vision come from? Aly's never seen the future before—only the past. At first she thinks the vision was a trick, sent as a distraction by the same person who killed her sister-in-law. But as she works to stop them, Aly discovers that her vision of Tony might not have been a lie so much as a premonition.

Buy now!

GET A FREE NOVELLA!

IF YOU SIGN up for my newsletter at www.adabell.com, you will receive *Mystic Treasure,* the story of what happened on that momentous day. Just a little gift from me to you.

After a busy winter of murder-solving, Aly can't wait to relax with some family fun at the Shady Grove Annual Treasure Hunt. For twenty-five years, town residents have searched futilely for a chest containing the deed to an abandoned mansion on the edge of town. At this point, Aly's pretty sure the treasure is a myth, but she's always up for Shady Grove shenanigans.

When the Treasure Hunt gets underway, a suspicious new resident throws everything into question. Someone's got a hidden motive for participating, and the town may be in danger. Can Aly solve the mystery to save the day?

MYSTIC TREASURE PREVIEW

TODAY WAS the perfect day to win a fortune. I wasn't the only one who thought so: The Shady Grove Town Square hummed with excitement. Fluffy white cumulus clouds peppered the sky. Between the slight breeze and the mercury topping out at seventy degrees, this was the kind of gorgeous summer day that made it worth living through the humidity and thundershowers.

Half the town must have turned out to watch this event. Granted, half the town meant a few thousand people, but still. Town Square was bursting at the seams. Set near the end of

Main Street, the largest park in town ran a block down to Second Street, with the other end across the street from City Hall. My three-year-old nephew and I stood under a tree, soaking it all in while we waited for my brother to join us.

Thankfully, Kyle hadn't yet seen the guy making balloon animals. On the corner nearest me, a marching band warmed up their instruments, complete with a bagpipes player. Town residents milled around, visiting the booths that had been set up to feed and entertain us. A huge banner extended across the square, welcoming everyone to the "WALTER SPARROW ANNUAL MEMORIAL TREASURE HUNT".

According to the rumor mill, Walter Sparrow was some eccentric millionaire who died about twenty-five years ago. Instead of leaving his money to a relative or a friend or a local animal shelter, he created this big annual party for everyone to try to win the big prize. No one had managed yet. My best friend Rusty suspected the entire story was a lie, and Walter just wanted to make sure we all talked about him forever after he passed.

Considering the amount of money supposedly on the line, I was surprised there weren't fortune hunters sniffing around all year, but Shady Grove wasn't like other towns. Maybe the same forces that led to unusual happenings kept outsiders away?

Or maybe our town was so tiny that no one outside a fifty-mile radius had heard of Shady Grove or old Walter? That was more likely.

Personally, I suspected Rusty was right. The whole thing sounded like an urban legend. An excuse for a big summer party, but anyone expecting to find treasure would be sorely disappointed. Still, we'd teamed up and gotten ready for action. The practice solving clues should come in handy once Rusty finished getting his PI license.

Tugging my hand, Kyle peered up at me with his big brown eyes and heart-shaped face from beneath his adorably oversized sun hat. "What's a treasure hunt, Aunt Aly?"

I resisted smoothing an errant chestnut curl that was so like mine. "It means Rusty and I are going to follow clues to find a lost item that has been hidden somewhere in the town."

"I find it! What did Rusty lose?" Kyle asked.

I grinned at the spark of excitement in his eyes and smoothed a curl off of his forehead. My nephew had been born with the power to find lost objects, a secret we preferred to keep from the rest of the world as long as possible. Psychic powers ran in our family, but we'd recently learned that some people wanted to exploit what he could do. "Thanks, Little Man, but this game is for adults only. Besides, in a game, it's not fair to use our special abilities to win."

"Cheating?"

"Yes, that's considered cheating."

"Oh. I won't cheat." Kyle stuck out his lower lip. Then his gaze landed on one of the tables below the "WALTER SPARROW MEMORIAL TREASURE HUNT" banner. "Cookie?"

With a laugh, I let him drag me to the table, manned by my friend and the owner of the local coffee shop, Julie Capaldi. A self-described "recovering lawyer," Julie was a blue-eyed blonde who'd moved to Shady Grove a few years ago to take over her aunt's business. She'd set out cookies for sale, but also —and more importantly—iced coffee.

"Hey! Looking forward to the hunt?" she asked when we got within earshot.

"You know it," I said. "Rusty's excited to practice his PI skills. I'm here to stop him from picking the locks of every store on Main Street."

She laughed. "He's going to be a great investigator. I miss having him at the cafe, though."

Until recently, Rusty had worked as the manager at On What Grounds?. After helping me learn to use my powers and solve a murder, my new best friend discovered his true calling. I often considered myself fortunate Julie hadn't banned me from her store when he left. Where would I get my coffee?

Then again, I suspected she had a thing for my brother.

"Hey, kiddo!" she said to Kyle before offering him a cookie. "You planning to hunt treasure today?"

"Aunt Aly said I was cheating."

My face flamed. Maybe she wouldn't understand him? Three-year-olds didn't have the best enunciation, and his mouth was full of cookie. I wasn't sure how much Julie knew, either about Kyle's abilities or mine. She certainly hadn't heard it from me, but small towns didn't have many secrets.

"Cheating? That's no good." She gave me one of those 'kids say the darnedest things' grins.

In response, I gave her the most innocent look I could muster. "We're learning new words this week. Anyway, are you entering?"

"No, I can't."

"Can't?"

She shook her head and laughed. "I did it last year. You're only allowed to enter once."

"That's odd," I said. "Kevin did it last year, too. I thought he wasn't entering because he wanted to spend the day with Kyle."

"That's part of it, I'm sure. But yeah, everyone gets one chance." She shrugged. "People with money are eccentric, right? It's Walter's estate, so he gets to make the rules. I'll send all my good vibes to you and Rusty."

At the mention of my partner, I turned to scan the crowd. With the pre-hunt festivities drawing to an end, Town Square had cleared out somewhat. A lot of people still stood around, but most moved to ring the center, where the hunt would soon begin.

About fifteen feet away, I spotted my friend Tiffaneigh Pratt talking to Brad Stevens. The three of us studied science together at Maloney College. She still didn't want to admit they were dating, but the two of them looked awfully cozy. Their matching bright blue shirts with "WALTER SPARROW HUNTER" on the back told me everything I needed to know about their relationship—and my primary competition. Tiffaneigh hated to lose, and she had some flexible ideas about what constituted fair and legal gameplay.

We'd need to keep an eye on her if we wanted to win.

Mystic Treasure is ONLY available by signing up for my newsletter - visit www.adabell.com to get your copy.

AUTHOR'S NOTES

This book was one heck of a journey for me, to be honest. Shortly after I started working on it, my husband started (then finished, thankfully) cancer treatments, my cat died, and my dad got sick. I lost my agent. It was rough going most of the summer. This book was supposed to be released in August. I had to push it back once, and I was worried it would have to go back at all. I apologize for the delay and I sincerely hope it was worth the wait.

Thank you, first of all, to Sara and Abigail for helping me get through May. Thank you, Tracie, Sarah, Kara, and Marty for everything. Thank you, Deana, for talking me off the ledge. Also, I would like a sweater. Sending love to Madz Skills for her proofreading and La Voisin Art for yet another gorgeous cover.

I hope you enjoyed this book. If so, please consider leaving an honest review on Bookbub or with your favorite retailer.

ALSO BY ADA BELL

Shady Grove Psychic Mysteries

Mystic Pieces

The Scry's the Limit

Sight Seering

Mystic Treasure (Book 3.5)

Seer Today, Gone Tomorrow

A SHADY GROVE CHRONOLOGY

EVER SINCE ALY moved to Shady Grove, life has been full of surprises. Here's a list of all of Aly's adventures, in chronological order.

Mystic Pieces: Aly doesn't believe in psychics. Too bad she just had her first vision. Her first instinct is flat-out denial. After all, science and magic don't mix. But when a man is murdered, Aly realizes that she may be able to use her strange new "gifts" to find the culprit. If she can avoid getting herself killed in the process.

~

THE SCRY'S THE LIMIT: Aly's just starting to get the hang of her psychic gifts when she literally stumbles over her favorite professor's body. She's devastated and determined to get justice. But with several people benefitting from Professor Zimm's death, how will Aly find the real culprit before they find her?

~

SIGHT SEERING: As a psychic who gains powers from antiques, Aly is ecstatic to be invited to an estate sale. It's only after she arrives that she discovers the estate's owner didn't die in her sleep—she was murdered.

~

MYSTIC TREASURE: Aly and Rusty are excited to participate in the annual Walter Sparrow Treasure Hunt. As the event gets underway, they realize that there's more to this event than meets the eye. Someone's got a hidden motive for participating, and the entire town may be in danger.

~

THIS NOVELLA TAKES place between the final chapters and epilogue of *Sight Seering*. *Mystic Treasure* is ONLY available by signing up for my newsletter at www.adabell.com. Thank you for hanging out with me!

~

<u>The Pie in the Scry</u>: After nearly a year, Aly's got a plan to bring Katrina's killer to justice. But before she and Kevin can implement it, she has a vision of someone murdering Tony, the bakery owner. As if that wasn't bad enough—the killer looks exactly like Aly.

<u>Mystic Persons</u>: Aly just completed the biggest spell she's ever attempted, with a little help. But the magic came with an unexpected side effect, and now she's got to figure out why there's a dead man in the bedroom before her parents arrive for their holiday visit.

ABOUT THE AUTHOR

Ada Bell is an award-winning and internationally best-selling author who thought that it would be cool to use a secret identity when writing mysteries. After all, who doesn't want a secret identity? She doesn't remember where the idea for the Shady Grove mysteries started, but she freely admits that Kyle is based on a certain precious toddler in her own life. Ada loves Scooby Doo, superhero movies, STEM heroines, and cake. Mmm, cake.

Find Ada online at www.adabell.com, or get access to sneak peeks, news and more by joining her Facebook group or mailing list.

BOOKS WRITTEN AS LAURA HEFFERNAN

Retail to Riches Series

A Royal Farce

A Royal Pain (coming soon)

Push and Pole Series

Poll Dancer

The Accidental Senator

The Gamer Girls Series

She's Got Game

Against the Rules

Make Your Move

The Reality Star Series

America's Next Reality Star

Sweet Reality

Reality Wedding

The Oceanic Dreams Series

Time of My Life

Standalone Women's Fiction

Finding Tranquility

Anna's Guide to Getting Even

Find out more at www.lauraheffernan.com.

www.ingramcontent.com/pod-product-compliance
Lightning Source LLC
Chambersburg PA
CBHW030622190726
48286CB00008B/2358